Sun River

Sun River

Stories

Ben Nickol

www.blacklawrence.com

Executive Editor: Diane Goettel
Cover and book design: Amy Freels

ISBN: 978-1-62557-712-2

Published 2019 by Black Lawrence Press.
Printed in the United States.

Grateful acknowledgment is made to the publications in which some of these stories first appeared: *Fiction Southeast*, "Opening Night"; *Hotel Amerika*, "Involvement"; *Redivider*, "Tenants"; *The Greensboro Review*, "Annika and the Hulk"; *Alaska Quarterly Review*, "Afterlife" and "A Kind of Person"; *Crab Orchard Review*, "Sun River."

For Amy

Contents

Opening Night

1997

The parents had been fighting, but the daughter had a play that night and as always with their fighting it was the children who realigned them, like the deep gravity without which galaxies disband. She was an aardvark. The daughter was, in the play, and now through the house the mother chased her daughter with the aardvark's head in her hands, its snout bouncing, trying to cap the mask on the little one's head. The father waited in the living room with his camera. It was just like his wife, he thought, to turn a goddamn photograph—one photograph—into an ordeal like this. Grab the girl, snap her picture, move on with our lives—that would've been his approach. He glanced at his watch. Finally the girl was captured, capped, and handed the spear she would wield at the play's climactic moment. The mother arranged her before the camera, beside the hearth, and backed away delicately, as if the girl were a fragile item that could tip over and shatter. She was such an item, in fact. And if the mother that night had grasped how truly fragile the girl was—how instantaneously her small form could totter, fall, and become a thousand scattered pieces never to be whole again—then there would never have passed a moment such as this one, where her nervous hands let go.

Flash.

The father studied the picture the camera ejected, flapping it in the air to help along the exposure. The girl's brother, the son, lay on the living room floor with Anthrax Apprentice filling his headphones. *The sky*, the song screamed, *the sky. The sky is on fire.*

The family got into the car and glided through the evening, late sunlight flashing in the trees. Glaring out at them, from the daughter's lap, was the aardvark's vacant head. The sun flickered in its eyeholes, as if some malevolence were awakening there.

What if I forget? the daughter asked her family.

You won't forget, the father assured her. Nor would she. She had only the line: "A deal's a deal, and those are my termites!"

But what if? the daughter said.

The father glanced at her in his rearview mirror. Well, he said. Then I'll buy you a dipped cone.

We were getting dipped cones anyways! the daughter protested.

Well, the father said. I guess you have nothing to worry about, then.

They turned into the parking lot of the school, where various parents in eveningwear were herding along titmice and flocks of eagles. The eagles caught the boy's attention. Those eagles are gay, he observed.

They are *not*, his sister said.

Son, the father warned.

They have mascara. They're very fashionable, the boy said.

The father again glanced in his rearview, but nothing serious was brewing between his children. They loved each other. He loved them. Their mother loved them and he and their mother loved each other, even when they were fighting. This much was clear: it was the four of them as a unified entity, set against everything else. He parked the car, and his daughter jumped out and ran ahead of the family, weaving through the parking lot, dragging her clattering spear behind her.

The show, as they had known it would be, was magnificent. Animals of all description, all armed and ravenous, whirled plotlessly toward a climactic showdown between the aardvark and the orangutan. When it was time for that showdown, the stage lights dimmed, and into a single glaring spotlight walked their furry daughter and the overgrown child who played the ape. For flanges, someone had sawed a football in half and strapped a lobe of it to each of the boy's cheeks. He had no lines to say. The only dialogue in the entire performance, in fact, belonged to their daughter, who now cleared her throat and pounded the butt of her spear onto the stage. "A deal's a deal," she cried. "And those are my termites!"

At her word, the lights came up and the full kingdom of animals cast aside their weapons and whirled and danced. From the wings of the stage flew volleys of small candy, Tootsie Rolls and Hershey's Kisses and things, that the animals fell upon and devoured greedily. *Termites!* bellowed an adult voice from offstage. *Termites!* the voice bellowed again, and more candy showered onto the scene.

The show was dazzling light. It was color and motion. The giraffes, as they chased the candy, trailed green streamers from their ears; the bats swooped in iridescent capes; a blue haze, suggestive of boreal fog, seeped through the gauzy scrim. And the parents and the boy, seated together in the auditorium, watched the girl who was their daughter and sister. She was having trouble obtaining candy. The getup made her clumsy. Dragging tail and spear, she waddled after one thrown handful, only to have it claimed by swifter beasts. She pivoted to waddle after another: same result. But the girl had been the star. She had delivered grand oratory. And her parents, poised together at the edges of their seats, wondered: What could be in our little girl that she finds desperate meaning in such nonsensical words? What feelings must burn in her heart, and where will her life bring her? Already, the truck that would claim the girl had embarked from its vague origins, and was barreling toward town. Its throaty engine screamed through its gears; its dim headlamps raced through black timber. But the parents didn't know this. They knew only that their daughter was a strange creature in a strange drama, and the vessel of an enigmatic future.

It happened this way:

The curtain fell, there was cheerful applause. The curtain lifted, revealing the bowing cast, and the audience exploded out of itself, whistling and screaming. Finally the children retrieved their weapons and tails and climbed off the stage to join their families. The aardvark's family celebrated with ice cream. And while placing their order, the father trusted his wife's eyes at the exact moment she trusted his. It was no more than that. Turning from the counter, the father saw through the window of the ice cream parlor the girl in her costume waddling across Sprague Avenue. At the opposite curb there waited some other animals, a pair of kangaroos, her costars. The father uttered something unintelligible, and pushed past his wife and son and through a crowd of strangers to the door.

They never identified the make or model of the truck. For all the police knew, it was welded together from parts, in a backwoods garage. And so, for the remainder of his life, all the father had of the truck was the glimpse he caught of it as he burst onto the sidewalk and shouted his daughter's name. The vehicle, he would later recall, had round, frogeye headlamps, and a grill like the cattle guard of a locomotive. There was no housing for the engine. It stood naked behind the radiator. The cab was entirely dark. The father's only impression, beyond these qualities, was that the truck had emerged from the mountains. He didn't know why he believed that, but he did. The truck was a malicious spirit. It'd slunk from the mountains, like a wolf, and like a wolf it had carried off a lamb. After some months of this sort of talk, the detective on the case had to explain to the father that he wasn't being helpful. Had the father seen a license plate? Could he describe the driver?

There was one thing the father knew: he oughtn't have shouted. That was why the little girl stopped. Then it happened. That was it: it happened and was done. And rather than screeching brakes, there was the roar of cylinders as the monster peeled away. Farther down, the truck fishtailed into the night.

Traffic in both directions froze, as if the universe had been paused. The only sounds were crying children and the father's soles beating the pavement. He hadn't seen where his girl had landed. He ran a ways up the street, then ran back. From the ice cream parlor, there spilled a throng of strangers; from the throng of strangers spilled the mother and son.

The family ran at confused vectors, searching the shrubs and, farther up, a weeded lot. They had no words to offer each other. They themselves might've been strangers.

A woman with thick spectacles eventually found the girl in some brush. The family heard the woman cry out. Each froze where each was standing, a lone pillar in those dark weeds. Then, as one, they fell upon the scrap of darkness where the woman was standing. People they didn't know crowded about them. Sirens wailed in the distance, and when finally the family looked up from the crumpled figure, and looked into each other's faces, they were, for each other, no more than dim memories of the loved ones they had been.

The police arrived, and must've radioed that the matter was decided; when the ambulance appeared, it was without lights or siren, and the EMTs as they stepped from the vehicle were shy. Damaged as she was, lifting the daughter from the brush wasn't a straightforward proposition. A policeman led the family aside. The father brought his wife and son under his arms, but no more than his arms held them. Driving home that night, after providing and signing their statements, the boy gazed out of his window, the mother out of hers, and the father watched the road. They arrived home and parked in the garage, the engine ticking as it cooled. They went inside, and their separate directions.

Assisted Living

The meeting to decide everything, the one where I sat with my Rottweiler attorney across from Gwen and her bloodthirsty counsel, and scrap-by-scrap we tossed our assets onto the table for the dogs to quarrel over like steaks—that meeting, which my Rottweiler had informed me there was no coming back from (if Gwen and I weren't getting divorced before the meeting, he'd said, we certainly would be after), was scheduled for bright and early Monday morning. The Thursday before that, I was sitting in our kitchen, or at least what would remain our kitchen for a few days longer, before becoming (probably) Gwen's kitchen. Birds swooped back and forth past the window. I thought about how nuts it was that Monday morning I was going to awake, yawn and stretch, and then venture forth into the day to have my life torn asunder. Divorce, I thought. Di-vortia, from the Latin *divortium*, meaning a parting of ways, a fork in the road. That was happening to us now, as it happened to so many couples. We now were a couple divorce happened to. "Huh," I said aloud.

I tapped my lips, gazing out the window. A parting of ways. Becoming apart. That always had been, to my mind, an intriguing obverse. First "a part," then "apart." With the "a" and "part" parted, it meant two things were joined. With "a" and "part" joined, it meant things were parted. It was the kind of mental fucknutting I engaged in when trying not to experience too deeply my pending divorce. "Words," I muttered, a squirrel outside tightroping along a wire.

The phone rang. I observed it curiously, as if ringing telephones weren't a language I spoke. I made no move to answer it. Instead, I tried to recall if that telephone always had been there. So far as I knew, we'd done away with our landline years ago. Perhaps Gwen had fished this phone from the trash and re-bolted it to the wall as an inscrutable, spiteful gesture? My wife, certainly, was capable of such acts. In her toolkit were all manner of gestures that no semiotician could possibly parse, but which I, her husband, was expected to understand immediately, and be shamed by.

On the umpteenth ring, Gwen appeared from the other room (rather than establish separate residences, we'd established, in one home, a viperous stalemate) and ran her gaze back and forth along the plane separating me and the phone. "Is there something about this you don't get, Mark?" she said.

"No one's calling me at that number."

"So just let it ring. Terrific."

She snatched up the receiver. The call lasted several minutes, and I didn't catch a word of it. Instead, I watched my wife's face: her mouth mouthing words, her brow cycling through expressions. That woman, I thought. That wife of mine, molting into my ex-wife. Until a few years ago, she'd been a beautiful creature. The skin under her eyes had been only faintly pouchy, which had given her a weary, despondent air that men (this man among them) pined for. Her figure had been angular and nimble, like a deer's. And now? Well, Gwen's posture was poor, and portions of her midsection lumped and bulged. The skin under her eyes sagged badly, and throughout her face ran awful, furrowed wrinkles, as if God had scored her with a box cutter.

Not that any of this mattered. We were old, Gwen and I. In fact, all that truly disturbed me about Gwen's decline was her eyes, which as the rest of her had softened and drooped had become sharper, more vivid and mad. What I saw in her eyes, those icy eyes, was my wife's hardened resolve. Despite all forces to the contrary—despite the inertia of our marriage, despite my pleading and reasoning—she would leave me Monday. It would happen, and I'd be alone.

Call concluded, receiver cradled, Gwen said, as if I'd been listening in, "Can you believe that? Is that not incredible?"

"I wasn't listening to your call, Gwen," I said.

She drew breath to speak, then let it out. "You're right," she said. She glanced around, patting her pockets. It was as if she were gathering personal effects for her departure.

"What do you mean, 'incredible'? Who was that?"

"Forget it," she said.

"No," I said. "I'm sorry. Come on."

Gwen smoothed an eyebrow, then twirled her hand, dropped it at her side. "It was Roberta," she said.

"Okay." Roberta was Gwen's dinosaur of a grandmother. She called now and again.

"She's getting married," Gwen said.

I tilted forward in my chair.

"I know..." she said.

"Married? *Mar*ried?"

"I didn't get all the details."

I stared at Gwen. Then, still staring, I dropped my jaw open and laughed and laughed.

"Goddamn it, Mark." Gwen looked off, pissed. "Can you just...can you be an adult?"

"That woman must be a hundred and eight years old!" I cried.

"She's a hundred and one," Gwen said, as if a hundred and one were a marriageable age.

"What I want to know," I said, "is who's slipping it in that old raisin?"

Gwen left the room. It was her right to do that, but there were only so many places she could hide from me. I followed her into the study, where she'd dropped on a sofa to read magazines.

"Is it a shotgun wedding?" I said. "Is Berta gone with child?"

"We're not talking about this anymore," Gwen said.

"Did you tell her to think this through? She probably feels giddy and everything, but marriage is a long road."

Gwen turned a page.

"You'd hate to see this go twenty or thirty years then fall apart. She'd be all on her own at a hundred and thirty-one."

I thought for sure that'd win a smile from Gwen, but it didn't. Her eyes glided down the page.

"When's the big day?" I said.

"Saturday," she said absently.

That made sense. We weren't going to see a three-year engagement with this one. "I can do Saturday," I said.

Gwen lifted her eyes. After a moment, she tossed aside her magazine. "Mark, you are not coming to this wedding."

"Oh, you bet that I am, sister. You don't get to tell me what to do."

Aspen Gardens Assisted Living Facility was a sprawling, single-level complex surrounded by vast parking lots and staked trees. This was my first visit there. Somehow, I'd imagined a stately campus of Gothic halls with high dormers presiding over manicured quads. There'd be bell towers, grottoes—Roberta Desmond wasn't the sort of woman I could imagine in undignified quarters. But Aspen Gardens, as we pulled up, appeared to have been constructed yesterday, and didn't appear resilient enough to last till tomorrow. The siding panels, for instance, were oversized for the walls they covered, causing them to bow in places and bulge in others. The trees on the property still bore, on their trunks, Jim's Home and Garden price tags. And not one of the trees, that I saw, was an aspen.

We parked by a white van I supposed was used for recreational excursions, and were exiting the car when Gwen said to me, over the roof, "You know, Mark, just fucking shut up today, all right? I don't want a word from you."

I hadn't said peep in an hour or longer, and didn't say anything then. Gwen marched into the building. I slammed the car shut and strolled after her, twirling my keys, whistling. It was a brilliant, sunny Saturday, a fine day for nuptials.

The lobby at Aspen Gardens, I saw as I entered and removed my shades, might as well have belonged to a free clinic in a blighted neighborhood. "Oh my," I heard myself say. The lighting was sterile, and was reflected in the dull sheen of tile floors. Noises rang off the floors—shoe clicks and PA announcements, the soft insistence of telephones. Gwen leaned at the receptionist's desk, interacting with a clerk. Snatches of their conversation pinged through the bad acoustics: "Roberta Desmond... guests... granddaughter..."

On one of the walls, I observed a series of incongruous prints. One featured a cowboy campfire, another a sailboat, a third a milk truck. The prints were discordant not only in theme, but in style and sizing—aligned on the wall, the three paintings resembled the randomized output of a slot machine try. And they were all the room offered by way of personality. The other walls were blank acreages of cinderblock.

In such conditions, one can't expect human endeavor to thrive. And it appeared that even Gwen's attempts at ascertaining the location of Berta's wedding were meeting with frustration. "Roberta..." I heard her tell the clerk, "... Desmond." For each of the letters in her grandmother's surname (which it occurred to me then was the surname Gwen herself might reassume in the coming weeks), she tapped a finger on the desk: "D-e-s-m-o..."

"Ma'am," the clerk said, lifting his hands for forbearance. "Ma'am..."

He was an apple-cheeked little eunuch, gesturing now at his computer screen. "Okay, Roberta's in the system. She's a resident here. Okay, we've established that. But events like the one you're describing require *scheduling*, and I don't see any..." He gestured helplessly at the screen.

I joined them at the desk. "What's the issue?"

Gwen looked me up and down.

"What?" I said.

"Would you butt out of this?"

My hands, like the eunuch's, flew up.

"This doesn't concern you," Gwen said.

I backed away, turning away, looking something like a toy getting flushed down the toilet. Gwen and the clerk resumed bickering. "Supervisor" was a word she returned to regularly.

The chairs in the lobby were rigid plastic with metal armrests soldered together. I sat in one, legs crossed, hands folded. This, I began to understand, would be a painful day for all parties. Except, I decided, for this party. For Ol' Marky. That's right: today couldn't touch me. I was here for a wedding. It was a Saturday spent in the company of a woman who was yet my wife.

"…supervisor…" Gwen said again. And again. A queue of strangers formed behind her, people sighing audibly, checking watches. The clerk, agitated, vanished into a back room.

From my disagreeable chair, I contemplated my wife, wondering if she might glance my direction. She did, but the look she gave me wasn't fond. She looked away.

To understand Gwen's distress that morning, you should know some things about her, and about Roberta, and what, years ago, passed between them. We'll start with Roberta, that old queen. As of that morning, the day of her centenarian wedding, Roberta's vitality was anyone's guess (I hadn't seen her in fifteen years), but maybe sixty years earlier, in New York City, the woman by all accounts was a juggernaut. She was senior editor at a multinational house in lower Manhattan—one of the first women to climb that high in that business, and the first woman period to rise over, say, stapler duties at her particular firm (Armour & Sons? Something like that, some good old boy outfit). Some astonishing gap—I forget how it was described—separated her from the next woman down the ladder. Or no, it was this: all the salaries of all the other women at her company didn't amount to half what Roberta earned, and what she made didn't amount to half what a man in her position commanded. Something like that, I don't remember the story. The point was, a woman in Berta's position was like a butterfly cruising at 35,000 feet keeping up with jetliners.

It's easy to imagine how such a woman would impress her granddaughter—and indeed Roberta eventually claimed broad real estate in Gwen's heart—but my wife's admiration was late in developing. The impediment was Gwen's father, Gary, Roberta's lone child by a third marriage, who didn't, to say the least, participate in the world's adulation of his mom. In fact, where Gary Desmond was concerned, his mother was an embarrassment and travesty. I never met Gary, but if Gwen can be trusted (she can), then he was a dull-witted, reactionary ass. At family dinners, he liked to expound upon the humble, subservient roles all members of society should seek out for themselves—men to the paycheck, women to home and hearth. He never mentioned Roberta except to reiterate, now and again, that she was an affront to wholesomeness and decency. "She's having her carnival now," he liked to say. "But that big top comes crashing down." When it came to parenting, not raising another Berta was Gary's sole ambition.

All this according to Gwen:

In seventh grade, when her visitor first visited, Gary had thrown out the box of tampons her mother had placed under the sink, and replaced them with thick, perfumed pads. They were disgusting, Gwen said. And humiliating. None of the pants her father allowed her were snug or revealing, but even through loose denims or tweeds, the bulge of her napkin was plainly visible. What's more, if she crossed a quiet room, her thighs' chafing *squish* was heard one wall to another. It all seems exaggerated, but Gwen isn't given to exaggeration. Once, she confided, she'd crossed a classroom, during an exam, to sharpen her pencil. Such was the racket emitting from her panties that the instructor, as Gwen returned to her desk, followed her up the aisle to ask politely that she not leave her seat again till the period was finished.

The instructor winced, then chuckled painfully. "Well. Don't get up till the bell rings, anyway." To hear Gwen tell it, the freshly sharpened pencil had remained freshly sharpened till the exam's conclusion. She simply was mortified. She could fill in not one bubble more.

"They're basic," had been her father's justification for the pads. "If I have anything to say about it, Gwen will be *basic* about this."

"About *this*?" Gwen's mother had screamed. At that point in their marriage, Tammy Desmond would still confront Gary. It wasn't like later, when she'd clam up and allow him the say of things. (Though this is all secondhand—I never met Tammy, either.) "Just what do you mean by 'this,' Gary? You mean being a woman? Because that's not very basic!"

As with many confrontations, Gwen overheard this from her upstairs bedroom. Though it didn't last long. Gary, unwilling to engage, simply waited in silence till Tammy shut up.

"It's *complicated*, Gary," Tammy cried, but no, he dwelled in silence.

Naturally, high school for Gwen was miserable. Chaperoned dates clear through senior year, a curfew at sundown. Upon enrolling in college, Gwen was so brainwashed that she couldn't have guessed with any accuracy what she wanted from an education, or from life, even if her opinion on such matters was sought, which it wasn't. The deal her father offered was this: two academic years. If she was engaged by year two, he'd fund year three. But any fourth year would be at her husband's discretion, and on that fellow's dime.

"He wants a scholar for a wife," Gary had said, "then that's his can of worms. I won't load that gun for him."

One peculiar trait of Gwen's brainwashing was that it disoriented her emotional compass while leaving her considerable intelligence, and cunning, intact. In other words, arriving at college, she succeeded brilliantly at the perverse enterprise her father had laid out for her. By her first midterm, she'd obtained a steady squeeze named Alex: an engineering student, an athlete, a Christian. By sophomore midterms, they were engaged. She even refused the proffered third year. They were wed. Gwen assembled a home.

Only in her mid-twenties did the gravity of this nonsense begin weighing on her. Her depression found numerous manifestations, but basically she just physically slowed down. At first, she'd woken early to prepare Alex breakfast and coffee. Now, she slept long past breakfast, past Alex's departure. When finally she did arise, it was to putter about the house with the television roaring. Then she quit bathing. The house fell apart. At most, she left cold cuts in the fridge for Alex's dinner, then collapsed into bed.

As of that juncture in her life—Gwen was twenty-four—the only Roberta Desmond narrative she'd heard had been her father's diatribes about wholesomeness and doomed big tops. Gwen had adopted this view of her grandmother. (On what grounds would she have rejected it?) But it was that year, at the nadir of Gwen's depression, that *Vogue* ran a profile of the legendary Roberta Desmond, Publisher. It was totally by happenstance that Gwen saw the article. The neighbor's *Vogue* was mistakenly delivered to her door, and fascinated by the magazine's glossy texture and colors, she'd begun leafing through it.

Gwen and I still owned, as of the morning we visited Aspen Gardens, several copies of that *Vogue*. November, 1978. We kept them on a high, clean shelf, and I can still picture clearly the article's opening fold. Page 106. You turn from 105, and it's like drawing back the curtain of a Victorian boudoir. Immediately, you're clobbered with velvet, baroque paintings, a four-post bed. Seated at the photograph's center, upon an ornately scrolled armchair, is Roberta Desmond. Even in 1978, she's quite old. Viewed as a whole, the photograph is not unlike famous portraits of George Washington. In fact, the oblique angle of Roberta's blanched features matches precisely the angle of our founding father's mug on the dollar bill. Across the bottom of the page, in engraver's type, are the words AMERICAN ICON.

To hear Gwen tell it, she stared at that photograph for an hour before realizing this was her grandmother. Then she read the article. Then she read it eight times over. Finally, bathing for the first time in days, she caught the Metro-North line into the city. One component of Berta's reputation was her 100% willingness to make even the most influential personalities in the literary world wait. And keep waiting. (Somewhere there's a printed account of John O'Hara waiting so long in Roberta's lobby that he falls sideways from his chair and cuts his forehead.) But upon hearing that her granddaughter was visiting, Roberta hovered out from her office like a gleaming apparition and announced to everyone present: "My little lamb. Escaped at last from the wolves. Everybody go home."

They ate lunch across the street, salads and breads. Gwen sipped tea while her grandmother mainlined gimlet after gimlet. Soon, Gwen was confessing all her life's disappointments, her depression. "Nothing amounts to anything," she said. "It's all just... sag. Everything sags. Another sixty years..." Before she could help herself, she was blubbering into her salad.

Roberta observed this spectacle pleasantly, nibbling a radish. She tossed the radish aside. "But darling," she said. And many times over the course of our marriage did Gwen recount with fierce endearment what Roberta said next. "Darling, I don't understand."

Gwen's sobs trailed off. "What?"

Roberta laughed. According to Gwen, the laugh was entirely unselfconscious, entirely unapologetic. It was a schoolgirl's laugh. A schoolgirl giggling at a pet bunny. "Perhaps," Roberta suggested, "you should do something that feels good. That would solve the, uh, not feeling good problem." They fell silent. Roberta dallied her hand at the waiter, ordering a fourth drink.

It was all young Gwendolyn needed. Within the month, she'd left Alex and left Connecticut. At Syracuse, she began work on a Cultural Studies degree. When her father interceded on Alex's behalf, Gwen wrote him a letter severing their ties. They never spoke again.

Syracuse was where I met Gwen. I was studying Literature, scratching my way toward a doctorate. We met in the fall on the walking paths of Oakwood Cemetery, which was a common destination for moody Humanities students. Gwen's red hair tumbled over her rust-colored cardigan, her svelte legs sleeved in rayon. What a sight. I'm not a shy man, but I approached her cautiously, as if her hair were truly aflame. "You're looking for someone?" I said.

She looked me up and down. "Absolutely I am not."

"No," I stammered. I gestured at the graves. "For a name. Are you...?"

"Oh." Gwen considered the nearest stone. "Well. They don't really have names anymore, do they?"

"That's a pretty bleak view," I said.

"I meant just the markers." We observed the stones, the faces of which were pocked and lichened, the inscriptions unreadable. "But what you're saying is true, too. Nevermore, you know? 'Though we beseech with bloodied throats / they breathe no reply.'"

Our two strolls through the cemetery became one. Mausoleums floated past, little stone angels. Leaves showered down, tangling like cinders in Gwen's hair. Soon, we were discussing our lives, or the lives we wanted, the careers. We hoped to be academics (a dream we realized, eventually). Gwen was reading Simone de Beauvoir, and had never appreciated—she gestured at the funereal monuments, at the spire we now approached—how alike to a penis virtually every built edifice was. Or she'd appreciated it, but only in her gut, never in language.

We walked in silence. I fumbled for words, for wit, anything, but then Gwen relieved me by saying, "I guess... give unto man what's man's. Even if it's the whole world. Personally, I'm finished with it."

"Finished?"

She eyed me, then watched the path bending into the trees. What'd sparked between us must already have been palpable, because Gwen at that moment chose to issue a warning. She'd been married, she said. Married and divorced, already, at twenty-six. And never again. She loathed marriage. It was unwise, unethical, it made people ill. I nodded thoughtfully, thinking: Well. The prospects here aren't very good.

But in this regard, if in no others, I am indebted to Roberta Desmond. Because by that time, Gwen was visiting Manhattan every few weeks, eating lunch with her grandmother, and at one such lunch, when Gwen mentioned the Literature student she'd met in a cemetery, the old oracle piped up and said (I'm told): "Cemetery! A Literature boy! Why, he must be sickly and heartbroken. Just marry that rooster."

"What?" Gwen said. "But I... whoa, whoa, whoa, hang on."

Owing to Berta's own four marriages, and four divorces, Gwen had assumed her grandmother detested matrimony as fervently as she did.

But Berta set down her drink, and flung her arms out grandly. "Love! God, just let it take you, sweetheart! Let it wash you to sea!"

For the second time in two years, Roberta had told Gwen all she needed to hear. That lunch was in January, 1980. In August of that year, Gwen and I exchanged vows on a dairy farm near Plattsburgh. In attendance were my parents and sister, and some friends and cousins. On Gwen's side, seated alone in a bank of white chairs, were Roberta and her assistant, Cedric, an intern from NYU. Thirty years passed, during which Gwen and I secured appointments at a college in Massachusetts. Gwen and Roberta fell out of touch, gradually, but it was obvious my wife never stopped thinking about Berta. In the articles and books Gwen read obsessively—and eventually in the articles and books she published—the class of woman Roberta belonged to was celebrated unreservedly: the enfranchised woman, the fearless vanguard of mid-twentieth century art, poetics and industry. Where my wife was concerned, there could be no discussion of these women without the fate of all women hanging in the balance.

So yeah: if Roberta Desmond, age hundred and one, was to enter into a fifth marriage, then it was critically important to my wife that the ceremony be dignified. It was bad enough that the venue was an assisted living facility, and bad enough that the facility lacked architectural virtue. Bad enough that the lobby was soulless, that the place smelled of bleach. On top of all that, Gwen didn't need some impertinent clerk telling her no wedding was scheduled for today.

The clerk reappeared, eventually, wearing an apologetic expression. Whatever news he bore was unpleasant, and I wouldn't have wished, at that moment, to be standing in his institutional sneakers, flat in the crosshairs of Gwen Ebner's fury. He made to speak, and at that moment, up the hall, a pair of doors flapped open, revealing behind them a plastic chair with festive balloons tied to it. The doors closed then flapped open again, and I saw on the chair a dry erase board with frilly lettering:

BERTIE AND FREDERICK! YAY!

10:00! GREAT ROOM!

The poor bastard delivered his message: his supervisor knew of no scheduled wedding. But he could help Gwen schedule one, for a future weekend, if she liked? She flew apart then, screaming at the kid, stabbing a finger at his face. For whatever reason, I let her go on awhile. I just had to. It was important that day, after all, that my wife's intentions meet with frustration. Enough frustration, and intentions can change. Minds can change.

Finally, I crossed the lobby to where Gwen was shouting, and touched her arm. She whirled on me, ready to give her husband some of it.

"It's over here," I said.

"What's over there? What're you saying?"

"The wedding. It's up the hall."

It was difficult to discern which qualities of the Great Room had earned it its "great" designation. The room wasn't large, which disqualified the word's primary signification. Nothing about it was illustrious, which disqualified the secondary. Truthfully, it was difficult to discern which qualities of the Great Room had even merited the "room" designation. There were only two walls, and no doors. Some misalignment of the Aspen Gardens floor plan had created an alcove where Wings B and C intersected. Beside which, on the wall, someone had nailed up a plaque: GREAT ROOM.

Within the "room," there was a television on a wheeled cart, a rack of folding chairs with A.G.A.L.F. stenciled on them, and a crate with a blue lid. There were no further objects there, nor any people. Nothing suggested that in thirty minutes, in that place, a sacrament would be conferred.

Gwen drifted toward the crate, and peeled off the lid. She knelt and inspected its contents. I was ready to believe this was the wrong room, that a space of more demonstrable greatness waited elsewhere in the building, but then Gwen lifted from the crate a sheet of construction paper with B + F = LOVE FOREV stenciled on it. Beneath that, the crate contained additional paper, along with scissors, glitter, bunting, markers, glue. "They just gave up," Gwen said. "They didn't finish."

She dealt the paper back into the crate, and rested on her heels, hands limp.

"You know, they've got a lot to keep track of."

She looked at me. "What?"

"I mean, Roberta can't just bring the place to a stop. They've got a lot going on."

"You're an asshole."

"I'm trying to help," I said.

"Yeah. I don't think you are."

Eventually, Gwen smacked her thighs. "Well. I've got to put this together."

"Okay."

"We'll start at eleven," she said. "That'll be fine."

"What can I do?" And somehow, it was a sincere question. Though if you've been there, you know: past a certain threshold, bitterness and selflessness interpenetrate in a marriage, and feeling one you might act on the other.

"Really?" Gwen said.

I nodded. "Really."

"Well. You could check on Nimma. Make sure she's ready."

"I can do that."

"I've got to spruce this place up."

Just like that, the bitterness returned. I wanted to tell Gwen: Check on Nimma your own fucking self. You want to live without me, live without me. But I left the Great Room, and wandered off toward a nurses' station. When I arrived, I found a malnourished kid with a spiky mohawk hunched at the desk like a *Lord of the Rings* creature. He wore earbuds, and was reading employment classifieds.

He looked up, plucked out the buds. "Yo. What's happening?"

I explained I was looking for Roberta Desmond. Instantly, the life drained from his face.

"Yeah," I said. "You forgot the wedding, huh?"

"Fuck," the kid said. Leaning over the desk, he peered up the hall toward the Great Room.

"Look," I said. "Between you and me, I don't give a shit. But where's Berta? I'm supposed to check on her."

“Is there anyone down there?” he said.

“Just take me to Berta.”

The kid looked like a shoplifter, which probably he was. Hands in pockets, swinging his head left and right, he slunk out from around the desk. “She’s up here,” he said.

After numerous knocks, and no answer, the kid unlocked the door.

Of course, Berta would be dead in there. The kid knew it, I knew it. Behind the door, in the darkness, the only question was the attitude in which we’d find her. Slumped on the toilet? Draped from the bed like a deflated wacky man? At the back of the room, two slats of light shone under the window blinds. In the second before the kid opened the blinds, I made out, along the wall, the rough outline of what we were about to see. Oh Jesus, I thought. The blinds sang open, admitting fresh June daylight, and the kid froze, hand grasping the cord.

There, bathed in light, sat Roberta in her wheelchair. In no way was she dead—I’ve discovered bodies before (twice, actually), and let me assure you: corpses are more composed and tidy. Even when someone’s died wretchedly, as my father did (a massive coronary), the remains exhibit a dried-out tranquility. Where Roberta was concerned, not a thing about her was tranquil, and nothing dry. She was slouched, and listing, her jaw drooping with the simple gravity of it all. From several points along her lip oozed cables of spittle, which terminated variously down her chest and belly. The room’s sudden brightness had affected Berta’s eyes not at all—they hung as ajar as her mouth, the light passing laterally through her milky sclera. Worst of all, the woman sort of wore her wedding gown. The dress was pulled over her, at any rate, or most of the way over her—it covered some of one breast, and none of the other.

“Uhh…” Mohawk said. He looked at me hopefully, as if I might spring into action.

“I don’t know why you’re looking at me,” I said. “I’m a critical theorist.”

The kid returned his gaze to the spectacle in the chair. “Well. It’s just… there’s certain stuff I’m not supposed to take care of. I’m not one of the medical dudes."

"Pal," I said. "I don't know what you're supposed to take care of or not. I'm not the goddamn Surgeon General. Let's just get one thing clear: the next person in this room who's doing something is you."

The kid stared at poor Roberta. Miserable Berta. While we'd been arguing, a series of glottal slurps had emitted from the woman's throat. New thicknesses of spittle hitched rides down the established cables, docking at her torso like gondola cars. "Maybe," the kid said, "it's not as bad as it looks?"

"You probably should start doing something."

The kid released the window cord. Approaching Roberta, head tilted inquisitively, he said, "I'm thinking maybe she's just not awake yet. Know what I mean? Waking up's a bit of a process."

"What I'm thinking," I said, "is let's just establish this woman isn't dying. Okay, let's get dying off the table, then go from there."

The kid crouched at Berta's knees, peering in one of her eyes and the other. "I don't think she's dying," he said. He tugged her dress down, so that it covered both breasts. "She just needs cleaning up."

"That's fine. That's good enough for me."

The kid stood back from Berta, pondering her awhile. He looked over his shoulder at me.

"I don't know what you think you're looking at," I said.

"It's a two-person job, dude. It just is."

"You'd better find somebody else then."

He didn't move, and I didn't move. Eventually, accepting some unspoken complicity, we settled together on Roberta's sprung furniture. I crossed my legs. The kid tapped messages on his phone. Berta stared.

The next person to enter the room was the nurse who, that morning, had neglected to give Berta her shot. "Oh, fuck me, fuck me," she said when she saw her. The nurse was a squat thing, chubby, with tattoos crawling from her sleeves, onto her hands. Dropping her clipboard, she squeezed past me to kneel at the wheelchair. "Bertie, honey?" She touched Berta's wrists and neck. "Bertie?"

The nurse noticed Mohawk. "She needs her shot, then let's clean her up."

I smiled at him smugly, but he didn't see me.

The nurse rooted through Berta's cabinets, producing a nylon wallet containing a row of thin syringes. She swabbed Berta's arm and slipped the needle in; Berta's expression changed not at all.

"Let's go," the nurse said, and with Mohawk assisting, they wheeled Berta into the bathroom.

Garment by garment, as I watched from my chair, they removed her clothing. A rank pile of it, fragrant with piss, accumulated in the doorway. Moistening washcloths, they dabbed at the poor creature's wrinkles. About then, Gwen walked in. She looked at me, then at the heap of clothes, at the commotion in the bathroom.

"What the *fuck?!*" she said.

The kid and nurse, kneeling at Berta with sleeves pushed back, looked up guiltily, as if they'd been caught at some mischief.

The shot was working. Berta sat almost perkily, grinning at the bathroom fixtures, her elongated tits participating in the bony symmetry of her arms.

"Nimma . . ." Gwen said.

"She's all right," I said, but Gwen wasn't listening. Shouldering everyone aside, she knelt at the chair, confiscated a washcloth. Inch by inch, she laved the skin of her old idol, whispering assurances. Years later, I'd sit in a park in Richmond, Virginia, watching a sculptor restore a Confederate monument. And I'd remember Gwen Ebner, before she was Gwen Desmond again, kneeling in that bathroom.

To Gwen's credit, the Great Room by 11:00 a.m. was earning its name. From the ceiling, she'd hung fusillis of gold ribbon. She'd strung bunting along the walls, and on each folding chair (arranged in neat rows), she'd placed a glittering paper cone with tissue blooming from it, a favor for the guests. For an altar, she'd drawn a bed sheet over the wheeled TV cart, and crowned it with a candle. It was a tremendous effort. Out of nothing, she'd improvised elegance.

Still, the ceremony was ludicrous. You couldn't have convinced me that five people in that room, bride and groom included, understood that a wedding was happening. For one thing, none of the guests actually faced the altar. The Aspen Gardens employees who'd wheeled these mumbling souls into the Great Room (disrupting, in the process, Gwen's neat arrangement of chairs) had relinquished their charges haphazardly, and left to see to other duties. There were maybe twenty guests, all told. They gazed about dreamily, each at a separate patch of room, like bewildered children wondering where the Easter eggs were hidden. Several of the guests weren't even wheeled fully into the room, or had pedaled themselves out of it and were coasting up the corridor.

The minister was late. A doughy man, a Lutheran, he arrived yawning with his neckband dangling from his shirt pocket. Pegging me for an alert mind, he introduced himself and offered, from the side of his mouth, a litany of unseemly remarks. "Should I," he said, "slip in some last rites while I'm at it? Save myself a trip?"

He said, "How many sets of dentures you think end up in the offering plate?" and "Say I wore a turban up here, think anybody'd notice?"

"Father!" Gwen called, making her way through the jumble of wheelchairs.

"You know what I mean?" the minister said, nudging me playfully.

Gwen installed herself at the minister's side, and gazed with him at the assembly. "Does this work for you?" she said. "In terms of a layout?"

"I believe so. Though let's keep a defibrillator on hand."

Without glancing at Gwen, I knew she was furious. What she wanted to tell this dolt was, *You can fucking go to hell then. And take your abracadabra with you.* But she bit her tongue. "Very good, Father," she said. She even chuckled.

I was quite impressed.

"I think," she said, "we can get started."

She walked back through the wheelchairs. The minister fitted his collar, and I arranged myself at the altar. Oh, I forgot to mention: having no loved ones present to stand for him, the groom, Fredrick Demakis, had tapped me as his best man. Rather, his nurse had. Fredrick himself wasn't fully aware of me. (Nor, as I've said, was he quite aware that this was his wedding.) Here he came now, his nurse wheeling him. She squared him to the congregation, and depressed his brake. With some difficulty, the man shifted in his chair and leered at his one-man retinue. "Who're you?" he wheezed.

He'd already asked me that once. I ignored him, and "Prince of Denmark's March" started up somewhere in the corridor. Soon, Roberta Desmond wheeled into view, riding her chair quite regally, quite fluidly, floating along like the ghost she resembled—like the ghost she'd nearly become, an hour earlier, like the ghost she indeed would become, two days hence, when she passed away in her sleep just forty-eight hours into life with Fredrick.

At the helm of the chair, guiding Berta through the confused guests, was my wife, my Gwendolyn. Behind her, marching in step, came Mohawk, holding his phone aloft, swiveling it side to side so people could hear the music.

Something happened—the music halted. Mohawk lowered his phone and popped around on it, dancing his thumb on the screen. Gwen waited, holding Berta's chair. Perceiving an opportunity, one of the guests shrieked: "It's just *splendid!* It's a *gorgeous* occasion!" Though I was confused as to how the woman knew this; her chair faced the wall, her back to the proceedings.

"Something with my data," Mohawk muttered.

Gwen dug in her pocket, producing her own phone. She hit buttons rapidly, then tossed the phone into Mohawk's hands. The march started from the beginning.

They came toward us, Berta now waving faintly, left and right, like a parade queen. The gown ruined, Gwen had dressed her grandmother in a plain beige pantsuit, in the tradition of first ladies. Like a first lady, Roberta also wore pearls and powdery makeup. When she reached the altar, I saw that the makeup was everywhere—makeup in her hair, makeup on her shoes. The important thing now was just to keep this moving. It'd be done soon enough. But God, she looked terrible. My thought was: Reptile. Prehistoric reptile, eyelids blinking from below.

"Freddie, it's me!" this American icon cried. "Can you believe today's the day?"

The old man, head bobbing, regarded this newcomer to the altar. His wobbling hand rose, indicating Berta with a gnarled finger. "Who's she?" he wanted to know.

After the ceremony, Gwen left the Great Room without dismantling one ribbon of the decorations. Let management deal with that. In the exodus of guests, several of the folding chairs had been knocked over; several of the wedding favors lay crushed on the carpet, in bursts of glitter.

I trotted after Gwen, and caught her elbow. She wrenched free and kept on up the hall.

Where she stopped, finally, was on a patio at the end of the C Wing, which she'd accessed through a door reading NO EXIT. I stepped out there with her. Cigarette butts lay everywhere, littering the vicinity of a sand-filled bucket. Gwen crouched at the wall, and herself produced cigarettes. It was her lately revived habit. Both of us, in Syracuse and after, had smoked like chimneys, but for our twentieth anniversary, a reciprocal gift, we'd quit. Now, she was at it again.

"Can I have one?" I said.

She tapped one out, and handed it over without looking at me. She placed the lighter where I could reach it.

We crouched there, smoking, gazing at the heat trembling over the field beyond the fence. A breeze kicked up, and I remembered smoking with Gwen Desmond at her apartment in Syracuse, off Comstock Avenue. Those had been cold winters. The pair of us, in ragged jackets, had smoked on her porch while snow raced past the eaves.

I said, finally: "Honey, I wish we'd give things another try."

Gwen squinted at the field. "You've said that before."

"I know. I just thought..." I shook my head. I didn't know what I thought.

"Do you realize," Gwen said, "they won't even live together? Bertie and Fred. They don't have any dual occupancy units. The guy said check back next year."

"I guess I just thought," I said, "you might've reconsidered."

Gwen watched me silently.

"After today, I mean."

This confused her. She hiked a thumb at the building. "You mean after that?"

"That's got to change things, right? I mean, you can't look at that and think . . . ?"

My wife watched me trail off. Then she gazed at the field. "That was a sad thing in there," she said.

"That's what I'm saying. I mean, doesn't that . . . don't you think . . . ?"

Gwen inhaled deeply, drawing the day into her lungs. The summer day. "Mark," she said. "I thought I did well in there."

"You did," I said. "You did. That's not what I'm saying."

Gwen considered her Winston. Finally, she dropped it in the bucket. "I suppose," she said, "we were asking different questions today."

"What?"

The breeze lifted, and I heard a highway somewhere out there. My wife was gathering her things.

Involvement

2002

Women are everywhere. They're never the same and never quite different. She wants her way, you want yours, and after some wrangling it fades. We call them "affairs" but I prefer "involvements." No one deserves "affair." It's a holy thing when people come together.

Mine have been women of all kinds. They've been students, whose involvements must adhere to theorems of modern love, whether theorems they've read or those they've concocted (though they can have trouble differentiating the two). I'll tell you a story about a student I was involved with. She was in attendance at a lecture I gave at Gonzaga, a lecture concerning contract law. It was the first year of her J.D. She sat at the front of the auditorium in a black sweater and black jeans, to set off her platinum hair and cherry lipstick, and throughout my talk she sat with legs tightly crossed and a scowl that said: "Everything you are, old man, has been explained to my satisfaction in sociological texts. Your every act masks sexual perversion."

I wasn't there to dispute that. I just wasn't so sure my perversions wouldn't entice her. After the talk, I walked off the stage and strode straight for her. The rest of the audience had risen and was filing out, but she remained in her seat with legs crossed, the toe of her boot carving little circles in the air. As I approached, some bubblegum inflated from her lips, then popped and was retrieved into her chewing teeth.

I said, "I've been watching you for about ninety minutes now."

Her eyebrows inclined, her chewing unabated.

"I'm just convinced you've reached conclusions about me," I said.

She shook her head. "No. You're a bright individual."

I nodded. "Uh huh."

"You clearly grasp unilateral covenants."

"And...?" I said.

"And... you're so sure you're big shit."

I laughed. She grinned, so that I saw into her mouth where the gum tossed like drying laundry.

"I suppose I'm such big shit," I said, "that I could tell you you're coming with me right now."

"You certainly could attempt something like that."

"And you certainly could comply. And you will," I said. And she did. And hearing that, you might think I "won" this exchange. After all, I was a middle-aged man privileged enough to fuck a girl born just four presidential administrations earlier. But there aren't winners in involvements. Rather, there aren't losers. Yes—absolutely I was fortunate to know that girl's body. But on her side, she got to affirm her view of the world. I'd made myself into precisely what she wanted, what she expected—though it's lewd to say, I'd arranged myself to fit the compartment she'd provided, and in this way the exchange was squarely balanced. As contracts went, it was perfectly elegant.

My other involvements have been artists, schoolteachers. I've involved myself with prostitutes, occasionally, many of whom could deliver their own compelling lectures on the matter of unilateral covenants. There've also been believers, who are wonderful. A believer withholds herself fiercely, desperately, and when her resolve finally disintegrates the sex is rapturous. She flings herself into fucking like a suicide from a bridge.

I'm 51 now, and involvements don't thrill me like they used to. For one thing, I've accepted their impermanence. The younger me expected each new encounter to lead somewhere enchanted and remain there—I've let go of that. Love, I understand now, is tidal, and flows out again. Still, every woman's somewhat new, and all are remarkable.

Kelly I met on a work trip. Then there was Tara, who served coffee at the bakery on 14th. Emma, Maureen. Today, as I sit on my balcony, I'm remembering Angela. We met playing rec league basketball, if you can believe that. It was the coed division. I didn't think at first it'd be Angela. I'd eyed another teammate, a twenty-something playing rec league to preserve some essence of intramurals. This one, Julie, wore goofy socks and pigtails and liked to cheer comically from the sideline. She had terrific joy and was fit without being pretty. There's agony in that, and agony stirs me.

I hadn't considered Angela's prospects until the night I saw her alone at the gym where I lift. From the weights, you can peer through a glass wall to the basketball courts below, and she was down there in the aquarium light, perfecting her jumper. She started close, in the key, and as I watched she backed out to midrange, and finally launched threes. If she missed she started over, and if she got through without missing she started over just the same, without ceremony. She was 40, maybe 45. She had graying hair, cut short and motherly, and a good build and excellent shooting form.

By the time I got down there, she was running dribbling drills. She drove right before drag dribbling out, then drove left and dragged out, again and again. I like that, when a woman's severe with her body. It's an invitation to be severe together, in the dark of a bedroom. Eventually, the ball hit off Angela's foot and bounced my direction. She ran over, looked up. "Terrific work," I said, handing the ball back. "You'd make a great rec league teammate."

She recognized me then, and was embarrassed. "I was just…" she waved a hand at the court.

"You were practicing."

"Yeah."

"Can I join you?"

She opened her mouth, but didn't speak. She seemed shy, but then maybe seemed inconvenienced.

"You know what?" I said. "Forget it. I'll be down here."

I took a ball to the other hoop, where I shot halfheartedly and watched her. Observation like that, after all, is powerfully sensual. She feels the man's gaze move onto her, as the man himself wishes to. It's only effective if she registers his gaze, however, and Angela was oblivious to mine. Almost immediately, she'd banished me from her thoughts and immersed in a drill where she shuffled along the baseline, passing at the wall. But that was sensual, too. A woman's indifference wrings a man like a sponge. I watched the ridge of her thigh as she powered along, the cocked hips of her stance.

When she switched to bounce passes, I interrupted and insisted on helping.

"I'm really all right," she said.

"You need someone passing back to you. Come on."

Angela rested the ball on her hip, regarding me wearily. No shyness there—she was annoyed from her Reeboks to her eyebrows. Irritation in a woman is off-putting, but only if one hasn't learned to stroll straight into the teeth of it. Do that convincingly, and pleasantly, and she senses immediately that you're impervious to her contempt, which, in the proper dosage, is potent medicine.

With a view to that outcome, I walked past Angela and, with an air of serenity, installed myself under the hoop, hands in pockets. Eventually, as I'd known she would, Angela drew a tolerant breath and shook her head. She crossed to the wing, and started whipping me passes.

I passed back, and she whipped more passes, and more, her absorption in the drill becoming so total that I could examine her body frankly, nakedly, as if through two-way glass. What I saw impressed me. The woman I passed to wasn't provocative, but stepping into her passes, her lifted shorts revealed straining adductors, taut as cable. Those muscles, let me tell you, weren't lost on me. After all, the same musculature comes under the same duress while fucking. It's the willing anguish of parted thighs. Angela bit her lip, perspiring, her fingertips seeking the ball's seams.

She'd have passed all night, had an attendant not appeared to say the gym was closing. We sat on a bench while she changed shoes, pulled on sweats, her atmosphere salty and warm.

"Let me take you somewhere," I said.

Her hands froze on her laces. Then she resumed tying. "I guess that was coming, huh?"

I laughed. "I don't make a secret of these things."

"These things?"

"Look," I said. "We'll go now. It'll be just a drink."

She cinched one sneaker, moved to the other. "I don't know if I like the sound of 'these things,' Greg. It's Greg, right?"

This sort of thing happens, and happens with men as often as with women. We grow too fixated. We trap ourselves in conventions and protocols, forgetting that, at our essence, we're brutish fauna drawing breath after breath, until another breath isn't permitted. For that reason, we oughtn't waste time obstructing ourselves. I allowed a silent moment—allowed Angela to reacquaint herself with bodily reality. Then I said, softly: "It's whatever you want. I just thought we'd pass an hour together."

The lights in the rafters were snapping off. Angela lifted her face, watching them. She nodded. "Fair enough."

There's a bar where most patrons wear sweats—even the patrons who haven't come straight from the gym, as most of them, it's plain to see, haven't. I met Angela there, and we ordered beers. She climbed onto a stool facing the bar's mirrored backing and I climbed, sidesaddle, onto the stool beside her, my gaze on her profile and my knees bracketing her leg. It wasn't the first time, in a bar, that I'd addressed myself to a woman in this fashion. And really it's hard to imagine a more advantageous arrangement: I observed Angela directly, at a near remove, while she observed me via the mirror. It excused us from eye contact, which is one sure method of unfettering a woman's urges. Our beers floated forward like candles. I rested my elbow on the bar top, my cheek on my palm, and regarded Angela thoughtfully.

She was, certainly, plain and of bland style. Beneath her motherly haircut, I noticed unpierced ears. Her fingernails, in her lap, were pared aggressively, to the beds. But also beneath Angela's short hair sloped an elegant neck I wanted to touch, and I liked her hands' repose in her lap, the self-possession of that. One of her hands rose, touching her beer glass, before retreating again. I did touch her neck then, lightly.

"No," she said, leaning away.

My hand floated midair, as if browsing Angela's neck for a nerve that might stimulate carnality. But I withdrew my hand, pivoted toward the bar. I sipped my beer. "You're something to watch on that court," I said.

"Well. Thank you."

"Where'd you play?"

"Excuse me?"

"You played college, I assume."

"Oh," she said. "No, nothing like that. I just play now."

I glanced at her. If anything's more bizarre than a middle-aged woman playing rec-league basketball, it's a middle-aged woman taking it up for the first time. But I'd have seen it if I were paying attention. Running her drills, immersing in that rigor, that repetition, Angela was lost not in routine but in discovery. The next question was why this discovery, why now? But new paths late in life seldom have happy beginnings. I asked, instead, "What do you like about it?"

"About basketball?"

Angela fidgeted on her stool, revolving her glass a quarter turn on its coaster, like a padlock combination. "I guess," she said, "I like learning it. There's little things, like how you think and move. You feel yourself get it right, you know? It feels good."

Till that point in the evening, Angela had exuded about as much warmth as a helmet-haired Puritan magistrate. But it was then, discoursing about basketball, that her carriage loosened, her breathing eased. Never let standoffishness fool you—there's a soul in each of us, once you break open the hard casing. Angela said, at a somewhat ardent volume, "And God, Greg, do you ever watch the pros? Steve Nash? He's so fluid, so... elevated. I mean, that I'm even capable of watching him—like, that my eyes even register his talent—makes me feel better about myself. It's like connecting with a higher species." She sipped her beer, sloshing it onto her chin; laughing, I walked down the bar to fetch a napkin.

"You laughed at me," she said when I returned.

"Well, you spilled."

She shot me a glance, the first playful glance I'd seen from her. Climbing onto my stool, I resumed my earlier arrangement, knees spanning the length of her thigh. "What else?" I said.

"What?"

"Tell me more about basketball. You're on fire with it. I'm loving that about you."

Her look turned suspicious. And it ought to have been suspicious—I'd caught sight of the warm-blooded thing living inside Angela, in her caves and tunnels, and I'd pursue that creature clear back to its den.

"What else?" I said. "Tell me."

"Well." She addressed her glass. "It's a graceful sport. I'm not graceful, but it lets me pretend."

"What else?"

"I guess . . . I like passing. Getting a pass right feels perfect. It's better than scoring."

"Well. I liked watching you out there."

She didn't know what to say.

"I liked watching you move. Your body."

She gazed at me. There was no further reaction, though—no barricades thrown up, no evasion—so I moved my hand to her thigh to feel the hard muscle I'd observed earlier. It felt as I'd expected: lean strength fanning down from her hip. But also her leg was tense. I withdrew my hand. "What?" I said.

"Greg. I want you to tell me something, and be honest. What are you trying for here?"

I laughed. "Show me a man who knows his own heart."

"Well. You don't have to know your heart. But I do."

I watched her a moment. Then—and whatever else you might claim about me, I don't think you could say I'm dishonest—I said, "I want . . . to get closer to you. I want to know how close we can be."

She rolled her eyes.

"You don't have to believe me."

"Look," she said, "don't put roses in your teeth. I'm not sixteen years old. I'm just saying, don't waste my time."

"I won't."

"If we're doing something," she said, "then let's *do* it. That's all I ask."

"We're saying the same thing."

She looked at me. She laughed.

"What?" I said.

She sipped her beer. "Whatever you say, Greg."

Given Angela's reticence, and her pragmatic mien, I'd have expected her behavior in the bedroom to approximate, more or less, an engineer's operation of a train—haul the relevant levers, till the cars lurch into the yard. That wouldn't have been terrible. I enjoy mechanical sex as avidly as other phylums of intercourse. All of it, after all, is naked spirits escaping the flesh, yet using flesh to do so. But the prudishness wasn't there with Angela—not hardly. As she dissolved into fucking, she became a creature of the discipline, utterly organic, an apostle of eroticism.

Actually, it was too much. It was comical. There we were, on the sofa in my condo. She swung a knee over me, and lifted her shirt off enticingly, inch by inch. Gazing at me from above, breasts flattened in her sports bra, she dangled the shirt behind her, like a stripper would, and dropped it. I laughed.

She flinched. "Don't laugh at me."

"Why? I can't be happy?"

We locked eyes. Eventually, thawing, she moved her pelvis to my mouth and arched back like I was a pommeled saddle. She tossed her hair, though there wasn't enough of it for anything to happen. I rose from underneath her, laid her down, removed her bra and panties. To accelerate things, and dispel the air of tortured arousal, I passed a flat lick up her cunt. Something like an ox at a block of salt. She recoiled, and I once more spread her flat, like smoothing stubborn gift wrap. I applied my tongue savagely, earnestly. She allowed, and even enjoyed this, but when her gathering pleasure grew too prominent in the room, and nothing could be heard but her hoarse panting, she pushed me away and scrambled down the sofa.

"Get back here," I said.

She did, but not without reviving her dramatics. With a snarling expression, lip curled, she crawled toward me like a cat keeping low in the grass. My patience with all this was waning, but for her own purposes, her own fulfillment, Angela needed to act this out. So I thought: Fair enough. Crawl around awhile. I let her purr. I let her, like the kitty she wished to be, lick at me here and there.

But that was done, it was my turn. Gripping her as if I myself were operating the levers of a train, I pressed Angela into the sofa, her face in the cushions, and took her that way. It was my fantasy now, it was *my* fulfillment, but beyond letting it happen, which was all I expected, Angela actually adopted my fantasy as her own. She bucked and grunted, describing for the night the acuity of her heat. She told me she wanted more of it. She asked me never to stop.

It was, I believe, the moment I began knowing her. And what I realized about Angela was this: she wanted less to fuck than to abandon herself to fucking. She wanted both of us, actually, to disappear into a moment, a shared conjugal dream.

But had Angela paid better attention, she might've realized I'm not a man who dreams anymore. Not about fucking, or about anything else.

By the end of that night, the militant Angela I'd observed on the basketball court had transformed entirely. Gone was her rigidness—she curled beside me, stroking my chest lightly, nudging my knee with hers. As if a switch had been flipped, she couldn't stop talking. She described basketball plays she admired, described her jogging route, nutritional habits. Speaking of, there was a restaurant downtown she suspected wasn't as good as the hype. Though we should try it sometime. That, or maybe this other place. Generally speaking, she enjoyed eating in restaurants even when the food sucked. How can you not have fun when a chef in a kitchen…

None of her talk was very inspiring, I'm afraid. (The restaurant she mentioned, for instance, was the kind of place anyone with eyes could see was a disaster.) But if she wished to pass an hour in conversation, I believed she should do that. I didn't have anywhere to be.

"This feels good," she interrupted herself to say. "It's nice just talking to someone, you know?"

We lay on my bed with the city's glow cast onto the ceiling above us. Past our toes, in the window, Spokane's unmarvelous skyline did its best. It was a junior varsity city with junior varsity architecture, though at night, swelling with lights, it became nearly more than itself. "Talk," I said. "Please."

She smacked my chest then, too pertly, and said: "What if I told you I was a mommy? What would you say to that?"

Why Angela would believe her motherhood was shocking news was anyone's guess. Anyone who reached our age usually had reproduced at least once. I myself had a daughter in Boise, an eighth-grader. If pressed to wager, I'd have bet Angela had two kids or more, maybe many more. The markings of it were plain on her body. And anyway, who cared? If children impeded our capacity to love and make love, who would ever have them? Rates of abandonment would skyrocket. In fact, the opposite was true: children evidenced our loving and fucking.

Angela fell silent, drumming her fingers on my chest. Then it was one finger tapping, and finally her hand lay still, like a faucet that'd dribbled off. "Connor," she said.

"What?"

"His name's Connor. My boy. He's a sweet kid, too. God, but it's frustrating." She sat up in the dark, studying me.

"Go ahead," I said.

"No, it's just…" She shook her head. She patted my chest once, thoughtfully. "It's not that I can't give him time, you know? I have plenty of that. It's just… he doesn't want it. Time's not what he needs, you know? He needs... something, and I don't have it. And he knows I don't have it."

She must've heard, at that moment, what she sounded like. Her chin dropped to her chest. She tilted her head back, examining the ceiling. "God," she said. "I'm sorry."

"No. You want to share."

She shook her head. "You don't need to hear this shit."

"I don't mind." And I didn't. Like I said, I had nowhere to be. And part of what Angela sought from me was an audience for her troubles—she had her audience, she should avail herself of it.

She went on. She complained about her husband, or ex-husband, whichever it was. He had no use for their kid, letting the boy stay at his place while never staying there himself, enabling all varieties of misbehavior. She confessed her loneliness, her fear of aging—matters that trouble us all. Matters that arrive at our doorstep like a package in the hands of an insistent courier; he'll be back tomorrow, and the day after, and day after that, until we accept delivery.

She bared her soul to me, and I listened. Though in the window, at the foot of Spokane's skyline, the Spokane River thunders through a deep gorge. And as Angela talked, I propped on an elbow, watching the mist of the river rise into the flood lights down there, under the city's old bridges.

It's the same view I'm contemplating this morning. One of the bridges, Monroe Street, is 150 feet high at its center. The vehicles crossing it are tiny as bugs. I understand that the city, every several weeks, sends policemen to talk jumpers off the parapet. When the police arrive, the jumpers often are barefoot, having left their shoes on the sidewalk behind them.

Well. We all have things we think about.

I should confess this about myself: I'm temperamental. Anyway, temperamental is how others perceive me when one of my moods strikes.

The moods don't feel temperamental. That word suggests vagaries of disposition, and my moods, all of them, are more unidirectional. It's as if, suddenly, the earth multiplies its gravity. I'm twice as heavy. My spirits are twice as heavy.

In the throes of my moods, I'm still responsible for my actions. That's an important point. Always, naturally, I'm responsible, any twitch of my nerves being a fiber in the weave of my character. (Though "responsible" oughtn't be confused with "remorseful"—no mature being is remorseful for his nature.) But I'll admit: while suffering from a mood, I'm given to behaviors others believe I'll someday apologize for.

I dropped Angela off, that first morning, at her house on Indian Trail. Later that week, I knocked again at her door. She answered wearing sweats, carrying a gym bag. "Greg!" she cried. She lifted a hand, then smacked her thigh. "Hey! Didn't know you were coming!"

Usually, I prefer cheer like Angela's. After all, all of us are vulnerable creatures, at God's whim—why not smile when chance allows? But that day, suffering from that day's mood, cheer was intolerable. It was repugnant, even. Hostile. Angela's smile was a vegetable grater on my skin.

Still, I try to retain my social delicacy. I gestured at the curb. "Were you leaving?"

"Oh." She glanced at her bag. "No. I was about to shoot hoops, but I—"

I retreated a step. "I'll call you later."

"No," she said. "Come in."

"I shouldn't interrupt."

Angela stepped back from the door. "Greg, get in here. The gym's not going anywhere."

I stepped past her into the foyer of her house. She closed the door, and we were alone in the house, a ceiling fan churning lazily. At that moment, I could've nudged from its pedestal the fluted vase standing beside me, and watched it smash on the floor and felt nothing in particular. I can't account for that. I'm not obligated to account for it. Angela slung her bag onto the floor. I said, craning my neck at the vaulted ceilings, "What a beautiful home."

She studied the ceilings with me. "It's too much. I feel like a pinball in here."

"No. You're more than a pinball."

Angela nodded reflectively. "That's suave, Greg. What a suave line."

We laughed, our voices resounding off the tile floor and ceiling. The little bursts of it—our chirps of laughter—were like so many birds swooping at my face; I wished to pluck them from the sky and twist their heads. "Can we," I said, "maybe drink something?"

"Oh," she said. "Okay." She glanced at her watch.

"If you don't want to..."

"No, I like drinking. Wine?"

She led me up the hall, past portraits of herself and the boy, Connor. He was an uncomely kid. I didn't enjoy the sight of him. We passed a portrait of a smaller child, a girl, cheesing at the camera with missing teeth. I didn't know who she was, but the sight of her stopped me short. Some aspect of the child's face, or of the photograph, emitted an eerie sorrow. I kept walking, being in no condition, that afternoon, to confront sad mysteries.

In the kitchen, Angela poured us saccharine merlot with no character whatsoever. It tasted like gumdrops. "This is excellent," I said.

She examined the label.

"You know," I said, "this is so generous. I'm interrupting your day."

"Stop it."

"I could've called..."

"Greg." Angela rested her hip against the counter, glass floating at her lips. "A girl learns to be flexible."

I raised my glass to that.

"What doesn't bend..." she said.

We sipped our dreadful wine. I stood quite close to Angela. I said, "I don't want to think about you breaking."

She laughed.

"I mean it." And I did. Such are my moods that any intimation of suffering shatters my heart with empathy, even as I would gladly, at the same moment, rake fingernails down my own mother's face.

"You," Angela said, "are full of lines today."

I placed my wine on the counter, to relieve the indignity of holding it. "I want to make you feel good," I said.

Her eye dimmed. "Is that right?"

With no haste, I pinched the zipper of her sweatshirt and drew it open, the garment parting like theater curtains.

"What's with you," she said, "and gym clothes?"

"Go in the bedroom," I said.

She held my gaze, tongue probing her inner lip. Eyebrow cocked, she left her wine and walked up the hall. I heard a door close.

Alone, I absorbed the room's stillness and silence. In the window, weak sunlight pooled in the yard, where a play structure stood in shoddy repair. I pitched my wine not in the sink but the trash, and followed Angela.

She waited in the bedroom, clothes removed entirely except for her gym shoes, which was an elegant touch. She'd crawled onto the bed and was gazing over her shoulder at me. "Is this what you wanted?"

Approximately. Though her presentation was vulnerable, and I wanted not vulnerable but illicit. She should've dished out her spine, like a swayback mare, and spread herself for me. Instead, just waiting on all fours, she was angular and soulless. If this were charades, I would've guessed: "Amish coffee table."

I loosened my tie, unfastened my cuffs. Angela pushed upright to assist with my shirt buttons, but I told her no. "Stay where you are."

When I was ready, I climbed onto the bed behind her and arranged her properly, like the mare. "What are you . . . ?" she said. "How are we . . . ?" She glanced over her shoulder, scrutinizing my intentions. She adjusted her hips, but it was an adjustment in the wrong direction.

"No," I said.

"What are we . . . ? I don't . . . ?"

"I'm showing you."

"Well, but you're not—"

Reaching up her back, I shoved her roughly into the mattress. "Like that," I explained.

"Greg..."

"Like this." Gripping her wrists, I pinned one arm to the mattress, then the other. She was a shackled mammal now, prostrate to the headboard. "Is that better? Is that fun?"

She replied, but I wasn't entertaining replies. Moving a hand to Angela's cheek, I held her face against the mattress. I began on her that way. Eventually, she worked her teeth onto one of my fingers and bit hard.

"Ah," I said, "all right."

She wouldn't release the finger, so I pushed more fingers into her mouth and held her chin like that, in my fist. "There we go," I said. "I don't have any problem with that." I jostled her chin, then jostled it hard, till her teeth released. "There you are." I patted her face. "That's not so bad. You can take that."

Well. No matter the tranquility of my conscience, I understand that many, even most people find this disgusting. To those people I say: don't be sentimental. It happens in involvements that parties cross the line. Angela'd crossed it when she treated me like a shrink, burdening me with troubles. Settling the score, I crammed my hand in her mouth. Trust me: when it was over, we both felt better. Debts were satisfied. I can't count the number of lectures I've delivered on the subject of breached contracts, and the opportunities they create. Bilateral opportunities. Such transgressions sever partnerships, or else deepen them. Thicken ties, compound obligations. That's all this was. I needn't be Angela's therapist; she needn't let me debase her. But we were exhibiting flexibility. We were strengthening bonds.

Afterward, lying in the sunlight filtering through the blinds, Angela drifted some distance away. She said, as if addressing the sunlight, "What was that? Why'd you do that?"

"I need to be quiet right now," I said.

I must've slept. When I awoke, it was dark in the room and Angela, wearing a bathrobe, sat in an armchair near a lamp. She gazed at the window, though the glass was black and showed only the lamp, and her sitting there.

"Good morning," I said. I felt considerably better.

She glanced at me, then looked again at the window. "Not quite morning."

I found my watch on the nightstand. It was eight p.m. "Could you eat?" I said.

Without discussion, we dressed and drove along county roads to the country club I frequent. Here and there, the Little Spokane River flashed in the trees, rippling through moonlight. Golf season was over, but the restaurant at the club was open and lively. We passed through the dining room to a table overlooking eighteen. Nearing the table, an acquaintance greeted me. "Hello, Counselor," the man said, and I shook his hand. Angela kept walking, not waiting to be introduced.

We ate a straightforward meal—crab bisque and small sandwiches—and through it all, she breathed not a word. The meal finished, table cleared, I dabbed my mouth and tossed aside the napkin. "Very well," I said. "What's wrong?"

Angela glanced at her hands, her pared nails, then folded her hands on the tablecloth. She gazed at eighteen, at the green, lying empty in the glow of the restaurant. "You're a taker," she said.

"What?"

"That's what you want. I asked you what you wanted, that night in the bar. You said you wanted us close, some line like that. That's a lie. You want to take things."

Another acquaintance of mine, a physician, strolled by and squeezed my shoulder. Angela didn't notice. Facing the window, she said, "I guess I don't blame you. It's common enough."

"I wish I knew," I said, "what you're talking about."

"I mean … no one'll mistake it for the highest species of love. But maybe …" She tapped the table absently. Then she stopped, finger pinned to the tablecloth. "Maybe it's useful."

Our waitress arrived, and I signed the slip and thanked her. To Angela, I said, "You're being pretty mysterious."

But she'd moved to a new subject. "Look." She tapped the windowpane. "Ducks."

A raft of them, maybe six, piloted small V's across the pond beside the green. "Out for a swim," I said.

Angela glanced at me strangely.

"What?"

She studied the ducks. "That's not swimming. They're looking for food."

Our next rec league game was Tuesday, but Monday night Angela came over. Frankly, it was poor timing. A client of mine was fighting a water rights dispute, and needed filings immediately. The information for his filings was scattered throughout my living room, its arrangement approximating its arrangement in my mind—my living room, that night, *was* my mind. Then the door buzzed, and everything lost coherence.

"Come in," I said, returning to my desk to finish an infringement notice. Angela dropped in a chair, disordering some folders I'd stacked on the armrest. I ignored this, kept working.

"I told him," she said.

"Your husband?"

This confused her, so she might've been divorced after all. I watched her over the rim of my glasses.

"Connor," she said.

"Who?"

"My son. I told him about us."

"Ah."

"It was..." She bobbed her head. "...difficult. I don't think he understands."

I scrawled out a note. "Why should he understand?"

Angela stared at me. I finished the note. "It's your life. Let him understand his life."

"Are you serious? Greg, he's my son."

I removed my glasses, placed them on my notes. What on earth Angela's son could *mis*understand, I hadn't the faintest idea. Two people with genitals wished to deploy them. If he could tie his shoes, he could understand that.

"He needs to know that his mom..." Angela stared into space, shaking her head.

I slipped on my glasses.

"Anyway," she said. "I'm not thinking about that. I can't think about it. You know what I need? You know what I really need, Greg?"

I typed some sentences. "Mm?"

"I need a vacation. Can we do that? Can we just *go*?"

I dropped my glasses on the desk. Going, truthfully, sounded wonderful. I'd go anywhere, right at this moment, if I could take these pages with me. If there could be silence.

"Have you been to Chelan?" she asked.

"Have I *been*? Sure."

"Let's go tomorrow. You and me."

"It's winter, Angela. That place is shut down."

"I know, even better. We'll be alone."

"We have a game," I said.

"What's one game? Greg, I need this. And I'll be honest: I need you to fuck me to pieces."

It was an odious remark. Needing it's one thing, but begging? Groveling? If you crave stimulation, with no mystery or wonder attached, no poignancy, stimulate yourself and leave me out of it.

"I'll take care of everything. Just meet me tomorrow, okay? I'll be at Campbell's."

"I'm not sure I can make it," I said.

"Yes, you can. I have a wet mouth that says you can."

My mood flared again, faintly. It was like a gray snowstorm gathering behind my eyes.

"I'm going home," Angela said. She was out of her chair, folders sliding to the floor. "Campbell's," she said. "Tomorrow."

***

Of course, I planned to stand her up. Things with Angela were burned out, and I didn't wish to blow on the embers by joining her for a romantic getaway. I'd let the ashes of our involvement cool, and scatter on the wind.

Plans are meaningful only to the degree that we know ourselves, however. I spent the following day sequestered in my office, placing calls, reviewing injunctions. I expected to stay there all night, but then was cruising west on Highway 2, snowy wheat fields racing away in all directions, the Cascades a ghostly wall before me. I don't know what changed my mind. Chalk it up to a sentimental twitch. Angela was a warm soul, and I thought maybe we could walk more miles together.

It wasn't to happen. I arrived at Campbell's, discovered Angela in the empty dining room, and she wasn't alone. Sitting with her, at a window table, was the slovenly boy I'd seen in the portraits at her house. He was skinny, with a broad face and poor complexion, his stiff bangs hanging flat, like broom straw. One dislikes kids like him. Their ugliness is flagrant; no matter how far you stand from them, they encroach on your personal space.

I lingered in the doorway, fingering the car keys in my pocket. But Angela noticed me, her face blooming into a smile. She leapt up, collected me by the elbow, and led me to her son. "Connor, meet Greg. Greg, Connor."

The kid paid her no mind. Instead, he balanced bread under his fingertip, like a football waiting to be kicked. He flicked the crust, twirling it. Angela rolled her eyes. "Fine, fine," she said.

We sat, at which point the kid lifted his eyes at us—just his eyes—before again watching the bread, flicking it.

"Greg's an attorney," Angela said. "And a pilot, too. He flew in Vietnam."

I didn't flinch, at least not obviously. But that wasn't information I'd authorized Angela to share.

"Why are you, like," the kid said, "reading off his résumé?"

I thought: Excellent question.

Angela laughed, nervously. She nudged her son. "I thought you'd be interested."

And I remembered then what she'd shared, that first night. He needed something, her boy did. Something she didn't have.

The kid removed his hand, letting the bread fall. "May I be excused to the restroom, please?" he asked, for some reason, in a cockney accent.

Angela gave him a look.

"If you please, I'd like to be excused to the potty, Mum."

"Connor..."

"Mum, the potty. Please, if you'd be so generous. It's mighty pinchy in me twinkler."

"Go," she said, "go, go."

"Tremendous merciful, Mum. Tremendous merciful." He wandered off.

The boy gone, I stared at Angela. She gazed past me at the dining room, hands limp on the table.

"Do you mind," I said, "telling me what's going on?"

"Greg..." She folded a napkin idly, turning its corners to the center.

"What?"

"This is it, all right? This is what I need from you."

She looked at me. I was silent.

She laughed. "Oh, that's great. That's rich."

"Now hang on..."

"You can't even give this, huh? Even this is beyond you."

"Angela, I don't know what 'this' is."

"It's help, okay? Just *help*, Greg."

Connor emerged from the restroom, examining the bric-a-brac on the walls back there. There were nautical ropes, a life preserver. He tugged one of the ropes. "You know," I said, "you shouldn't ask for too much."

Angela stared at me.

"Ask for too much, you won't get anything."

"I," she said, "didn't ask for any of this."

Connor returned. Angela watched me, face blank, then with effort produced a smile. "And how was ye piss, then?" she asked her boy.

"I don't know why you're using a funny voice," he said, again fiddling with his bread.

I watched Angela. And at no other moment in my life have I seen, on one face, such sheer fatigue. But she drew breath, and it was as if by inhaling she swallowed her fatigue like a stone, or sword. It's what separated Angela and me. As needed, she could escape herself into something new. Whereas I can't. Or won't. I've always been just the one thing, and being one thing there can be, for me, just one escape.

Her face playful, bright, Angela balanced some bread and flicked it into Connor's lap. He tossed it back at her. The restaurant was dim and silent; in the window, wearing its choker of cabin lights, lay a black lake a thousand feet deep. A waiter appeared, yawning, and before he could speak I pushed back from the table. The three of them watched me, the waiter's expression concerned. I wished to say something, something about debts canceled, claims absolved. But if that was true, it was true without my saying it. I left. Outside, traffic lights swayed in the wind. My car waited on a deserted street.

Anyway, that was Angela. I never saw her at another game. Whatever's become of her, I hope she made peace with her boy. And I hope, someday, she appreciates what passed between us. Time with people, however brief, is precious.

Tenants

It was a little cabin across the lake I was refurbishing to rent during the summer. They say you can do that using computers now, without going through an agency, and I don't tangle with computers but the librarian in town showed me the program and it looked manageable enough. All I had to do first was fix the cabin. The carpets needed tearing out and things were water damaged, I had to retile the bathroom and kitchen, things like that. The computer the librarian showed me had another program for matching paints, and one where you switched out appliances, to see how they looked. It was like that machine could imagine every house that ever could be.

I don't know how the girl found the place. It was April, and the job not near finished, and besides the librarian I hadn't told anyone about my plans to offer a lease. But crossing the lake one morning, in my putter boat, I saw her Mercury parked by the cabin, under the cottonwoods there. There she stood, in her red coat, her little one squatting on the beach, splashing the water with his hands. What probably happened is I'd posted the advertisement on that computer, when I'd meant just to save it so it wouldn't go anywhere. Anyways, there they were at the cabin, at dawn, steam coming off the water. The kid was maybe three, and the Mercury was an old Monterey, which had been quite an automobile years ago, but wasn't now.

I slowed the boat, my wake running ahead of me onto the gravel, making the kid jump back like the lake had bit him. He was a cute little termite with blond hair. "Good morning!" I called to the girl, and she waved before tucking her arms back together. I dragged the boat ashore, and took my tools and such out of it.

"I'm sorry to ambush you like this. I tried to call," the girl said.

I tried to remember if she was one of the moms from the golf course down the lake. Sometimes they brought their kids around to my beach. But it was too cold for swimming, and I'd have remembered that Monterey.

"I hope we're not too late?" she said.

"Late?"

The kid ran down the shore, and she ran after him. Carrying him back, she said, "If we're not too late we can pay today. I have money."

I laughed, but felt bad because the girl seemed to think I was laughing at her. "Look," I said. "I have to admit, I don't know what we're talking about here."

"Is this not it?" She looked at the cabin. "It's how I pictured it."

"Wait, you mean to . . . ?" I said. "No, ma'am, I'm afraid that's not going to be possible. This place isn't ready. It's a holy mess."

The girl walked past me. "It looks ready. It's beautiful."

I can tell you this: people in this world have different ideas of beauty. Kids in town, at the library, I've seen with enough metal in their ears and noses to make a magnet salivate. And they have paintings now that're just messes of color, no form in them at all. But that cabin, I swear to you today, wasn't beautiful. It had ragged siding and yellow windows, not to mention the wasp nests everyplace, and the deck had enough cant to it that a damn banana'd roll from one end to the other. And that was the exterior. The interior was where the problems were. "I don't think you'd like living in this place just yet," I told the girl.

"Well," she said. "It needs cleaning. Every place does."

"It's more than cleaning," I said.

She looked at me. "I mean it, we can pay. I have money."

To prove she didn't want the place, I let her inside and showed off the mildew in the bathroom and the filmy drapes you'd get oily fingers from touching, the dust an inch thick on everything else. I'd lifted half the carpets, and yanked out insulation. The air in the place was so swampy I wore a surgical mask just to work there, which I took from my pocket and showed her. "Come back Memorial Day, you can have it the whole summer. Longer than that, if you like," I said.

But it was like a spell had come over her. She crossed the room to the windows, stepping around carpet tatters and buckets, and looked out at the sun on the water, or what could be seen of it through the grime. She said something I didn't catch, as I was watching her kiddo to make sure he didn't step on rusty objects, or mistake insulation scraps for cotton candy. "What?" I said.

"I bet it's good swimming water. Like it'd be cool on hot days and warm when it's raining."

She was right about that, and I said so.

"Brandon loves swimming. He'll do it all summer."

"Well. Place is yours if you can wait for it."

The girl looked over her shoulder. "You're sure it can't be today?"

It was like we weren't standing in the same building. Shoot, there wasn't anywhere she could've put a suitcase down.

"Listen," she said, "we need somewhere to go, and this is it, I feel it. I told you I have money. Can't we just move in?"

"If it's the lake you want," I said, "there's other places. You don't want to live in this junk. It's probably not even legal."

But her heart was living there already, and leaving would've meant leaving that. "Please?" she said.

A pair of wasps walked up the windowpane behind her, but there wasn't any use pointing them out. "There wouldn't be any privacy," I said. "I'd be in here working."

That got the girl excited. "Brandon's got daycare," she said, "and I'm getting a job. We won't even lock the doors, you just come right in."

"I don't know," I said.

The girl dug in her purse, and took out a checkbook. It must've been that I'd posted the advertisement, because the check she wrote was for the amount I'd stipulated. She started a second check for the deposit, but I stopped her. "You can forget that. You leave something other'n how you found it, I'll consider it a personal favor."

I gave them some days to settle in, inasmuch as that was possible. And that was fine, I needed a break from working. Labor like that, construction labor, fatigues me like it didn't used to. Somewhere along the line it's like my joints and back organized a union, and now any job not suited to their tastes, they all quit all at once.

From my place, across the lake, I could see how things came along for my new tenants. That first night, I saw just one light in the window. It was cold, and I couldn't remember if I'd turned on the cabin's heat. Then I remembered there wasn't heat in the cabin, not yet. I thought I should take some blankets over, but decided if I tried to make the cabin livable, I'd wind up doing nothing but that work, dawn till dusk. Then I remembered: making the cabin livable, dawn till dusk, was exactly what I'd been doing when Miss Red Coat in her Mercury came along waving a checkbook. So I supposed, far as discomfort went, she lay in a bed of her own making.

In the morning, I took my thermos onto the dock, sat in my chair, and threw a line for smallmouth. Boy, but it is a nice lake out there, I'll tell you what. At that early hour, little coils of steam lift off the water, like springs poking through a mattress, and there's trees along the shore, the sky's blue. You see eagles and osprey, and now and again a moose and her calves swim from one shore to the other, their ears up like sails. From my dock, the cabin the girl rented was a white-and-blue box tucked in a grove of cottonwoods. It was far enough off I could cover it with my thumb, but I could see what went on over there, and sound on that lake carries crisp as a carrot. The first thing I heard that morning was the screen door slam, and here comes the girl—Wendy, her name was—carrying her kid out to the car. The engine started, and that old Detroit chariot glided away through the trees. Well, I thought that was that. I decided I'd rip up the check she'd written me.

They came back in a few hours, though. Wendy propped open the screen door, and started carrying in groceries. She even had her little termite hauling things—I saw cans tumbling from his arms. They ate breakfast in the yard, and at one point waved across the water at me, the pair of them thrashing their arms like castaways. After breakfast, Wendy opened the cabin's windows and doors, and soon was carrying out trash bags to pile by her car, her arms stuffed in yellow gloves. Lord knows there was trash enough in that cabin to fill those bags, but also I hoped she wasn't throwing out my supplies and such. It got hot, one of the year's first hot days, and I went in. Come lunchtime, I heard screaming. Peering out the window, I saw Wendy and her boy splashing in the water, in bathing suits. My, but that takes courage in April. I don't care how hot it is. And I'll admit this outright: I lingered at that window awhile. I'm too old to get any ideas about a young woman, but being old means you've lived some, and from living I can say that it's sacred, a girl and her kiddo splashing in water.

They left that afternoon, and came back near evening, when I was on the dock again. Strapped to the Mercury was a dresser and mattress, and in the trunk, the lid lashed down, were chairs and things. I knew I should putter over and help, but it would've been ten minutes before I got there, and plus, as I mentioned, my vitality was on strike.

Though I don't think I'd have helped them anyways, even if I could've gotten there, and even if I were younger. Most women, most situations, you lend a hand, sure. But a woman can hold her head in just such a way, and carry herself in such a way, that says: I'm doing this alone, this is mine, butt out of it. It's a kind of marching, is what it looks like, and it can be seen from as far away as a lake's far shore. Though who knows: as a younger man I might've inserted myself anyhow. Some things, other people being one of them, you have to grow old and lose before you understand very well.

Wendy carried herself that way for a week or longer, wiping windows and sweeping the deck, and even raking last year's leaves while her son played in the piles. Then a morning came she walked to the car in a blouse, skirt and heels, holding the little one's hand. His other hand gripped a lunchbox. I supposed he was starting daycare while she hunted up work. When they didn't return, I loaded my tools and puttered over there.

As promised, the door was unlocked. And nothing I'd been working on was disturbed one iota. Wendy'd just dusted and scrubbed, and cleared out trash. In the bedroom, she'd made a space for their double mattress. The stove wasn't operational, but she had a hotplate in the kitchen, and in the yard I found a bucket for washing pans and forks.

It was a reasonable little home. I strapped on my kneepads, and yanked up carpet.

We got along into May, them leaving in the morning and me fixing things, then in the evening them returning while I packed my tools, and made sure the living areas were clean. One night as I loaded the boat, Wendy brought out lemonade and we visited while little termite chased minnows with his hands. Another night she made egg salad, and sent me home with sandwiches.

I did wonder about the dad, where he was, but I don't pretend to know how people should live, and I know there's women who mother alone, there always has been. Nothing new under the sun. Still, I wondered about that dad. Another thing not new under the sun is people come back for their kids.

When he did show, I knew it was coming from the change in Wendy. She'd stopped talking to me much, those evenings we crossed paths, and one evening from the dock I saw her come onto the deck alone, and lay arms on the railing and her head on her arms. She stayed that way till dark. Maybe she was tired—Lord knows she worked hard—but there's a tired that comes from working and a tired that's being harried by thoughts. Some days later, there he was. Wendy'd gone to work alone, and late in the morning a man came into the yard with kiddo running ahead of him. He watched his boy throw rocks in the water.

I gave him a day, but summer was coming and I can't work in heat. So the next morning, I loaded my tools and puttered over.

I didn't try the knob. I knocked respectfully, then knocked again, hearing footsteps patter around. The door opened, and there was Brandon holding a jelly donut, filling smeared on his mouth. Behind him stood a fellow with blue eyes, blue as the kid's, and a face dark with stubble.

"Can I help you?" he said.

"I'm here about the house?"

"Oh, of course. Howard." He pulled back his son. "Come on in, there's coffee."

I had my gloves on, and wanted to get started tearing apart the shower, but there's no shower on earth worth turning down a kindness for. Or worth turning down coffee. The young man set chairs by the window. "Sit, sit," he said, crossing to the kitchen. There was an attentiveness about him, and a delicacy, that reminded me of someone, though I couldn't place who. He ran water into the percolator, and shook grounds into the basket. "Pretty basic contraption." He held up the pot. "But it works. Best coffee I've had."

While the coffee percolated, he helped his son halve muffins, then instructed the boy to carry me one. "You take cream?" Before I could answer, he fetched cream from the cooler and brought it over, stood it on the windowsill. As a man, he seemed peaceful and satisfied. "Tell you what," he said. "Let's try outside." We dragged our chairs out into the grass, the boy jumping at our ankles.

Chris was the man's name. He settled into his chair, cupping his mug. Wind moved in the trees. "Well, tell you what. You've got a nice place here, Howard. Wendy and I, we talked about it. Place like this is all anyone needs."

"I'm glad," I said.

"And you live . . . ?"

I helped him locate my place, which was green with a corrugated roof. Mine's a handsome cabin, with trees around it and water in front, and Chris appreciated that.

"It's funny, isn't it?" he said. "We think we need so much. Then we find a good place and that's enough. We just live in it."

I thought about that. It was true, but also a place wasn't a life. Good as any place was, if you weren't good in it hard times came knocking. Like as not, they knocked at your door anyway.

The kiddo drifted off, checking for bugs under rocks. We watched him, the way men watch something while visiting with each other. Then Chris said, "Well, Howard, you must think we're fuckups. Wendy and me."

That startled me. I hadn't thought that, though I knew people could believe their worst parts were visible to everyone around them. "No," I said.

Chris stared at his coffee. "It's fine. We have had our problems."

"No shame in that."

He looked at me. "We're getting better, Howard. I'm getting better."

It's hard to respond when a man discusses himself earnestly. I nodded.

"I have to remember I don't need much. Air to breathe, is all. Just that."

The kid brought over sticks for his dad's approval, and I thanked Chris and stood. It was time to strip the shower tile, and clear out the backerboard and pan and such. Showers are a one-man job, in tight space, but when I stood, Chris stood with me. He said he'd pitch in.

"Oh," I said. "Well, all right."

"I'm not very handy. But I can do basic stuff."

"It's all basic. Basic stuff added up to a mountain."

"I like that," he said.

Inside, I handed Chris my chisel and got him going on the tile. As he'd said, he wasn't handy. He tapped at that chisel like a sculptor, little fine raps, and still, every few strokes, caught his thumb with the hammer. But he was attentive, and useful.

Toward the end of that morning, as we fitted the new shower pan, I realized who he reminded me of. It was my friend from Parris Island, from training there. Frankie Barton. Frankie wasn't violent—he was a Quaker, actually—but he couldn't hold a rifle without worrying he'd shoot somebody with it, or shoot everyone, and not from inclination in that direction, but, as Frankie put it, from potential. It was there to happen, he said, and so it might.

Now, Chris didn't resemble Frankie. Frankie was fair-skinned. But they both had a way, where everything they did started in their eyes, with a decision, then traveled out through their fingers, real deliberate and slow. Frankie'd stare at his hands. He said he needed to watch them so they didn't hurt people. They required, he said, 'round-the-clock supervision.

Chris mentioned looking for jobs. He said he wanted simple work, maybe landscaping, something where the sun beat down on him. Most mornings, though, he liked watching me work, and chipping in where he could. He wasn't skilled, but gradually he became more skilled, hanging drywall and caulking things, measuring with precision. Soon, I'd even have said Chris justified his presence, especially where heavy lifting was concerned. I'd even have said we became partners. Friends, even. We drank coffee each morning before raising our tools, then drank lemonade when it was hot. Like friends do, we teased each other over mistakes, like the day my hands shook mounting curtain rods, and I dropped three woodscrews into the toilet, one after the next. "Howie," Chris said. "If you don't like these screws, let's just go and get different ones." Another morning I was late getting there, and Chris walked onto the deck, waking the whole lake with his shouting: "Howie, God darn it, let's *go*!"

I work alone just fine, and even enjoy it, but working with a friend brings satisfaction no solitary endeavor can match. I was glad Chris'd turned up. Wendy was glad, too, despite her look on the deck that one evening. Things can go that way, where what breaks your heart also mends it, until you're not quite sure of the difference. They might go that way more often than not.

My only complaint with Chris was he accelerated the job, and I didn't want it to end. In June, with the finished cabin closing in around us, my impulse was to toss a hammer through the wall, or drop more screws in the toilet, anything to buy us more time. Buy me more time. But what can you say, that's things. Stay as close as you can to what brings you joy, so that when it's gone you know you weren't wasteful. Anyways, it's still a good feeling, finishing a job. The last detail was screwing light bulbs into fixtures, and Chris did that. Wendy was home, and Brandon, and the four of us made a ceremony of it, Chris screwing in bulbs while his boy tested switches. The last one: a success. We blew kazoos, then went on the deck, where Wendy grilled burgers. The lake was full of ski boats and bass fishers, loud music. It's a time of year I feel curmudgeonly, what with everyone on vacation and me just this dried up fossil in his putter boat. But sitting with those young people, that family, the lake was as much mine as anyone's. Tell you what, I was a proud old man.

Chris was proud, too. I watched him ease back in his chair, heels on the railing, like a fine gentleman surveying his lands. Brandon crawled into his lap and curled there. Wendy brought more burgers. To eat, Chris fed his arms under his son's, reaching his mouth over the boy's head. By God, they were a happy family.

"Howie," Wendy said, sitting beside me. She patted my hand, and you never remember how old you are till a young woman's hand touches your own. "Thanks for this," she said. "For everything."

"I should thank you folks."

"Well, that's ridiculous."

"She's right, Howie," Chris said. "That's absurd."

Brandon said it, too. "Ubscurd," he said.

I wanted to explain, to say how Chris'd given me company and coffee, free labor, how Wendy and termite brightened my days, but the kid saying "ubscurd" deflated all that. We laughed together.

"And actually..." Wendy glanced at Chris. "We have something we want to ask you, Howie."

Chris pulled his heels from the railing and sat upright, scooting Brandon off his lap. "That's right. We do."

My heart liked to have dropped from my chest. I just knew they were leaving, that this was it, I'd never see them again. Stick around long enough, that happens plenty: you lose something at the moment you start loving it.

But it wasn't that they were leaving. Instead, Chris hitched his chair forward. "Howie," he said, rubbing his hands. "Wendy, she's doing great at her job. They're thinking next month they'll move her upstairs."

We looked at Wendy, who shrugged shyly.

"And me," Chris said, "I heard about an interview. That golf course down there hires maintenance guys. It wouldn't be much, but add that to Wendy's..." Brandon wandered off, and Chris jogged after him. He came back carrying the boy in his arms. "Anyways, what I'm saying is we're doing all right now, me and Wendy. And what we were thinking, if you're open to it..."

He'd gone on too long for Wendy. "Howie," she interrupted, "we want to buy the cabin. If you'll let us."

"That's right," Chris said. "And I guess the point I was making is we don't have a down payment. But if you could take what we've paid so far, and maybe keep in mind that I've worked on the place..."

I couldn't have heard better news had I written it down and had them read it back to me. Them buying the place was perfect. It was like them renting, except they couldn't leave. And money didn't matter. I hadn't thought about money in years.

I told them yes, that was wonderful. I'd be honored to be their neighbor. Wendy, she just clapped her hands on her mouth and screamed. Chris smiled and nodded, then nodded more. We hashed out details, how they'd pay rent till August, then that'd be a down payment and we'd sign papers. We shook on it, and Chris set Brandon down to scoot him inside. "Go on in," he said. "That's your house, little buddy."

In the living room, among the furniture Wendy'd arranged (she'd furnished every room, hauling in chairs and lamps just as soon as we cleared our tools), Chris popped sparkling juice and poured it in champagne glasses. Brandon got some in a lidded cup. We toasted, hugged each other, and toured the finished cabin. Wendy served cupcakes she'd baked, which she said were for celebrating if I said yes, and eating their sadness if the answer was no.

I'm a perceptive man, I think, but it wasn't till Chris poured me more juice that I realized, of course, what his history was. As can happen, seeing juice in his hand was an observation that connected earlier observations, bringing them sense, the way you can stare at the night sky then suddenly see a constellation. Don't ask why I didn't see it earlier. I should've, as Lord knows I've had tribulations with drink. Most people do, sooner or later. But, I suppose, they were a beautiful family. And none are so blind as those who won't see.

They can keep not seeing, even after they know better.

July arrived, and things across the lake, to my judgment, remained peaceful. I didn't visit the Sauders as much, with the cabin finished, but every few days Chris appeared on the deck and pig whistled, and waved his arms till I started over in my boat. We ate lunch, or showed Brandon how to hook worms and cast. Some nights I ate dinner with them.

The first thing I had to intentionally not see was most mornings, at eight o'clock or so, Chris came into the yard with Brandon running ahead of him, and sipped coffee while his son played. Nothing amiss about that, except I knew people who'd worked maintenance at golf courses, and eight o'clock was in the middle of a shift. So Chris hadn't landed the job, or had but wasn't going, neither option being encouraging. The money wouldn't have mattered. Those jobs don't earn much even if you do show up. But I know what work means, and what not having it means, especially to someone in Chris's position. I didn't admit it then, but that entire month I was waiting for something bad to happen.

There's shouting of all varieties at a lake in the summer, most of it kids on inner tubes and older kids flying off rope swings, but the shouting the night it started at the Sauders' was different. I was in bed, and the shouting was part of my dream, but then the dream faded and the shouting kept on. I went onto the deck in my robe, and saw lights on at the cabin. Chris and Wendy stormed around in there, Wendy grabbing her hair and Chris hammering the table with his fist. Their screaming was why screaming like that is called "swearing oaths." I couldn't hear specific words, but understood they were vowing things, what they refused to do or would do forever. Between tirades I heard Brandon crying, and it must've been some crying to carry over the water. Then a door slammed, and the Monterey fired to life. Its headlights flew through the cottonwoods and up the road, but I was still awake later, when the car returned, shut off, and things were silent.

The next day I didn't see the Sauders. It was the day after that Wendy went to work, taking Brandon with her like she'd done originally, before Chris turned up. I sat awhile on the dock, fishing, and was there when Chris wandered into his yard. He sat in the grass without waving, or even glancing my direction.

There's scarcely a problem in this world you can't make worse by offering unwanted advice, but I thought if I made space for it, Chris might somehow help himself, without me speaking a word. I loaded tackle into my boat, along with lemonade and sandwiches, and puttered down the lake before puttering back again, trolling line up the opposite shore, like I'd just so happened on my excursion to pass my friend's yard. "Well hey, Chris!" I shouted, working my reel.

His elbows hung on his knees. He squinted at me, against the sun, not replying.

"Why don't you hop in? I've got lunch," I said.

He squinted off at something else.

"Come on," I said.

Chris got in the boat, eventually, and eased himself down in the prow. I moved off from shore, where the fishing was bad but where my friend couldn't change his mind and hop out onto land. He hadn't been drinking, I don't think. It wasn't that kind of pain, not yet. It was the kind where you forget there's other kinds, worse kinds, and where if you're not careful you'll throw yourself into the furnace.

"Take that rod. We'll catch dinner," I said.

The rod lay beside Chris. He studied it like it was miles off, like no way he could reach it, but then took the rod, uncaught the reel. He tossed his lure into the water.

The lake was still, the air still, there wasn't a sound and it was hot. The boat drifted, me casting now and again. Chris stared at his slack line. Young man, I wanted to say. You very young man. Hold perfectly goddamn still, do you hear me? Hold still, this will pass, you'll go back to your wife and kid. You son of a bitch, this can be your best moment or one you regret forever. You hold perfectly goddamn still.

And Chris did, rod in his lap—for an hour or longer, he held still—but it wasn't the abiding stillness a man in his state requires. Instead, it was the stillness of a young fool waiting to be set loose, so he could do what he'd known all along he'd do—long before getting in my boat, probably, and even long before meeting me. Before knowing such a place as Lower Twin Lake existed, and before knowing he'd need that place, badly, and actually acquire it, against the odds, before throwing it away.

You get older, and less is new, but there are things that never mind how often you see them, never cease to break your heart. And one of those things is a man taking a drink, and waking up in terrible shame. He sees his drinking as one thing, and his life as another, and resolves to stay in that life, which he's discovered is beautiful. He pushes at drinking like how he'd push at a wall, until the ground shifts under his feet and his life becomes the wall, and his drinking what he pushes with. Until it works, and he's alone.

Chris reeled in his line, and stowed the rod. He squinted at the sky. "Well, time for me to head in."

I saw the Sauders just one other time. It was late at night, as I was reading in my chair. There're these novels, by this old timer Vardis Fisher, who actually was a relative of mine by some connection. I like his stories, which remind me that whole lives were lived in this part of the country—long lives, that during the living may've seemed like they'd continue forever—before I even, some eighty years ago, drew my first breath of this world. Sometimes, I don't even read the stories. I just hold the crumbling paperbacks, which reminds me of the same thing. Anyhow, I was reading by the window when out on the water, in the dark, I saw the running lights of one of those houseboats people get drunk on and play music. It was strange, because the room where I sat was reflected in the window, and it was like the boat's lights floated through my house. I heard music playing, the low thump of it.

Such boats aren't uncommon in the summer, especially on weekends, but when I looked again I saw it was moored at my dock. That'll happen. People'll tie off somewhere and disgrace someone's land, leaving trash around and hollering. It's a circumstance I don't mind being curmudgeonly about. Laying aside Mr. Fisher, I went out on the deck. But before I could shout at the boaters, the music quit and someone shouted at me.

"Howie! Is that Howie?" To someone else, the voice said: "I think that's him."

Liquor skews a voice, but it was Chris. Out in the dark, I saw him climb off the boat, hitching one leg over the gunwale, then the other, like he was topping a fence.

"Hurry up," someone else said. "Get him or don't, but let's *go*."

"Howie!" Chris called, trotting up the ramp with his head down and hand raised in greeting. His head was down because he needed to watch his feet, which liked to have danced out from under him. Someone on the boat laughed. Finally Chris was in the grass below my deck, standing in the light falling out from my house. He shielded the light with his arm, which further troubled his balance. "Howie, it's you! Come on, I met these people. It's the best day of our lives!"

"Guy must be ninety," someone said.

"Howie," Chris said. "Hey, come on, man. And hey, get a load of this."

"Fuck, there he goes. There he *goes*!" someone said.

Spreading his palms before him, like he was creeping up on a rabbit, Chris heaved his legs into a handstand. His momentum carried too far, and he fell badly on his shoulder. The folks on the boat howled at that. "Goddamn it," someone said. "I won't watch that again. I just won't." With that, the boat eased back from the dock. Chris scrambled to his feet. "Hey!" he shouted. "Where you guys going?"

"Hurry up," someone told the driver.

"Hey!" Chris shouted. He tore down the dock, but made it only partway before he tripped, stumbling just far enough after that to strike his face on a cleat, which made a sound. He fell in the lake. His friends on the boat appreciated that, laughing to high heaven. To their credit, they did come back for him, and help him aboard. "I'm fine," he kept saying.

Even in the dark, even with him wet, I saw the blood spilling from Chris's forehead. His friends waved to me, apologizing. The boat moved off.

It didn't go far. It stopped at the Sauders' beach, and when it left I saw my friend wading ashore, then staggering through his yard. He fell in the grass, unmoving. The porch light snapped on, and Wendy, hugging herself, came out of the house to inspect her husband. Then she went in.

He was gone from the yard in the morning, and the Mercury was gone, and I never saw it again. Chris's own car, a Honda he'd bought for driving to work, was there a few days before it left. I watched the cabin that week, and nothing moved over there but some curtains fluttering in a window they hadn't shut. Each night, the same lamp glowed in the living room, still as a painting. One morning, with it starting to rain, I put on a slicker and went over there to shut that window. A note hung on the door with "Howie" written at the top, and "sorry" littered throughout the paragraphs so many times I quit reading. I still haven't read their note.

Inside, it was like the Sauders had stepped out to the park, or maybe to church. Shoes lined the baseboards by the door, and the kitchen sink had dishes in it. On the bathroom counter, I saw an open tube of toothpaste with the cap nearby. A wind kicked up, hissing the cottonwoods outside, and when I shut the window the only sound was rain pecking at the glass. The sill was wet, so I found a towel and wiped at it. I lost myself in that work, then turned and saw everything again, the home where they'd lived.

And isn't that it? Isn't that our years? Lives don't end, I don't think. They exist whole, from the moment we first imagine them. It's we who end, who fall from our lives and can't get back to them, who are reminded forever of what's sailed on without us, without a pilot at the helm, without passengers.

Sandpoint

I was in the bedroom folding clothes into a bag, and my wife Amanda had already stormed from the bedroom after failing to reason with me, then stormed back in and out again. She made salient points, but they weren't particularly inventive—I'd already considered what she was saying and decided what I had in mind to do was more compelling than what I stood to lose by doing it, which was her and our son, Knox, and the wholesome glow of our days together. Not small potatoes by any means, but not enough. I folded shirts and sweaters into the leather valise I used for work trips, not that there'd be any more work trips after this. I was abandoning that, too.

For all the screamed invectives and fists raining down on me, it actually had begun as an ordinary day. Amanda's and my two phones, charging on the dresser, had broken into song simultaneously at 6:00 a.m., as they did every morning. We lay still, as if the shrill music would sniff through the room, and not finding us return to what hellish cave it'd emerged from. It didn't—it kept sniffing, sniffing, sniffing. We threw back the blankets and swung our feet to the floor, and for an additional minute sat on the bed with our backs turned. Amanda's alarm was "electric swing," while mine was "jazz club;" you might say those divergent preferences communicated deeper divergences, a philosophical misalignment that could engender a separation like the one we were careening toward, that very day (though we didn't know it). But when I think about that morning, I think less about ringtones and more about our positioning: Amanda on her side of the bed, me on mine, each facing a separate wall. A couple positioned that way, I think, isn't ready to be tested.

I dressed Knox for daycare. Amanda, in the kitchen, hauled bagels and yogurt onto the table, creating a breakfasting station we could visit en route to the door. Work that day was forgettable: emails, calls, crawling from conference room to conference room. After work, I leafed through mail while fixing a cocktail. Amanda, upstairs, jogged on the treadmill. Knox dragged his little chair into the kitchen to sit with legs dangling, watching me. I tossed aside the mail. "You ready?" He nodded wildly, like he was riding a wagon down a flight of stairs. I opened the door, he bolted into the yard. It was our tradition, each afternoon, to spend time outside hunting robins. Knox believed he was a bushman in Namibia, and that the birds were rhinos.

It was six-thirty on the most pivotal day of my life, and nothing had happened yet. I relaxed in the lawn watching my son harry prey, the little birds hopping neatly aside as he flung himself onto the grass they'd vacated. Amanda, in the upstairs window, trotted swiftly, ponytail whisking her shoulders.

I even was content, if you can believe it. If somewhat dull, my life was prosperous and tranquil. No part of it spleened me, unless you count money and the years flying by, but everyone meets with those troubles. If you'd have asked me that evening how many more days would pass exactly as that one had, I couldn't have conceived of a number high enough. Knox was just four. Amanda and I were thirty-four. Our domestic arrangement was just getting underway.

The number flashing on my phone wasn't one I recognized, which usually meant I'd ignore the call. For whatever reason, that day, I answered. Of all people, the voice on the phone was Nicole Thorpe. Nicole Thorpe, after all these years.

"Oh," I said. "Hi."

Pleasantries were exchanged, but she got down to business. As she put it, the heavy things in her life weren't worth carrying anymore. She planned to drop them. She wanted to know: What was my story?

"Story?"

Knox dived at a robin on the far side of my chair, high-centering himself on my knees. I shifted the phone, helping him slide into the grass.

"I'm saying," Nicole said, "let's go someplace."

"*Go?*"

She laughed. "You know what I'm saying, Steven."

Knox skipped through the yard. Amanda stopped running, toweled her face. It was September, sunlight filling the trees, and I waited for what resolute virtue ought to have anchored me then. But I wasn't anchored, and virtue was a fantasy. And if this devastated my family, so too would it carry me beyond my family, where their devastation couldn't touch me.

"Steven?" Nicole said.

"Where?"

I'm not naïve. Fifteen years had passed since I'd seen Nicole, and I knew the woman meeting me at Yoke's Market in Sandpoint wouldn't be the girl I'd bid farewell to at Starbucks in Eugene, with her life barreling one direction and mine another. As I think about it, that day in Eugene actually persists fairly whole in my memory. We got coffee, and sat in Nicole's Celica to talk. Across the street, some bums at a bus stop drank from bottles wrapped in newspaper, gesturing the bottles and dancing. I wanted out—things with Nicole were picked over. And, it turned out, she was just as finished with me. We laughed about that, sipping our mochas and enjoying the bums, who seemed from our vantage to dance on the Celica's hood, just for us. In the fall, Nicole was transferring to Whitman, in Walla Walla, where she already was fucking guys. And me, I'd fucked a day earlier someone from Poly Sci 202, whose icy gaze and crisp features made me feel dangerous. As if in proffer, Nicole and I confessed our infidelities simultaneously, and laughed and hugged. And actually fooled around some, right in her car, my finger hooking into her desperately—so desperately it startled both of us. But that was it, and our coffees finished, we said goodbye.

And now I sat in my car at Yoke's Market in Idaho. And no: the woman meeting me today wouldn't be the girl I'd left at Starbucks. But it wasn't the point that she be that girl. The point was she carried that girl within, like a lantern housing a flame, and so even if Nicole'd taken a bad turn, into an awkward shape or poor complexion, or any other of the depredations we all make bad turns into eventually, there'd still be proximity to that girl, and that was magical. Opportunities like that didn't fall in your lap every day; whatever Amanda thought, it was worth what one paid for it.

I sat in my car in the parking lot, sipping coffee and every few minutes peering in the rearview at the cut over my eye, which a diamond I'd purchased ten years ago, on installments, had inflicted last night. It wasn't painful but was bleeding. A smaller cut adorned my cheek, and bruises purpled my arms and shoulders. Presenting myself in such condition was regrettable, but I hoped Nicole would see in my wounds the treacherous country I'd braved to reach her. A Nissan cruised by—she'd said to watch for a Nissan—but it was just teenagers inside smoking cigarettes. Across the valley, wet clouds left scraps of themselves on the mountains. The highway traffic sprayed tall fins of water from standing puddles, and in nearer puddles I saw the rain starting again.

A second Nissan passed, but turned out to be a Mazda. Then a Nissan with Oregon plates pulled off the highway.

It'd been seventeen hours since Nicole called asking to meet—seventeen hours of no sleep, suffering beatings, and driving 400 miles. There'd been time for this to sink in, this sudden new life, but none of it meant anything till that white Nissan parked across from me in the rain. Its wipers danced, its headlamps illuminating threads of water on my windshield. I couldn't see her in there. Then the door opened, and her door left open Nicole dashed to my car. It was locked. She danced small circles in the rain, like Knox when he needed to pee, and finally I found the switch. She fell in beside me, hair pasted on her face and jacket wet, all of it exhaling a freshness that'd been missing from my life for too long. She was ravishing. The girl I'd loved was there, encased in a woman anyone with a beating heart would've dropped his life for.

"Oh my God!" she screamed. "Steven!"

"Nicole," was all I could say.

"Jesus, what's this?" She climbed onto her knees on the seat, studying the cut over my eye. Her hair dripped on me. I laughed. "You didn't think this'd be free, did you?"

"*Yes!*" she cried, and we laughed and kissed. Her car stood across from us, headlamps shining, wipers thrashing, door open in the rain.

The place we found for ourselves was a bungalow college students had leased for the summer, and left in dubious condition. It was shabby, but we could move in that day, and if our definition of "furnished" wasn't too strict, it was furnished. There were florally upholstered sofas, and wooden lamps unmatched to the wooden coffee table, which wasn't matched to the end tables, which weren't matched to each other. The bedsprings fairly creaked from laying eyes on them, and even with the lamps in every room switched on, the place was gloomy: low ceilings and grimy windows, beyond which drooped fir trees, gray weather. But outside it was raining and inside it wasn't, and the baseboard heaters ticked to life, cozying things up. Carrying Nicole's bags from her car, the house with its lighted windows looked inviting in the dark trees. We switched off the lamps and fucked on musty quilts, a leaden dusk gathering around us. We discussed ordering food, but not a muscle in either of us stirred. We slept till morning.

When I woke, sunlight streamed over the house into the trees in the window. Across the street, children waited by a mailbox, faces in the sun. A bus arrived to carry them off. I was tired, but it was mellow, tranquil fatigue. In the kitchen, I found Nicole with coffee and rolls.

"There's my fuck slave," she said.

"Good morning."

Her blonde hair fell about her shoulders and chest, and she wore jogging shorts, a sweatshirt. When we'd known each other before, there'd been too much decorum to say "fuck slave" and such things, but we were past decorum, and past most else, and could speak as we liked. "I hope I didn't tear you up too bad," I said.

"That? That's tearing, in your book?"

I walked behind her, tracing my fingers along her neck, and sat down to breakfast.

"What do you think?" she said.

"I think we did the right thing. People should be happy."

She eyed me funnily.

"I do," I said. "You only get one go-around."

She laid a hand on the table between us. "Steven, I know we did the right thing. Or I don't care that we didn't. I'm asking what you think about the *food*."

"Oh!" Inspecting the roll in my hand, I said, "These are very fine. Delectable."

Her hand remained where she'd placed it, finger tapping the table. Then she withdrew her hand, leveling the finger at me. "None of that."

"What?"

"We don't need you sword fighting with your conscience."

"What?" I said. "No..."

Her gaze lingered on me, then shifted to the rolls. She sorted among them for one she liked.

"My conscience is clean," I said.

"These rolls," she said, "are what all rolls aspire to. Look." She turned her roll in the light, as if admiring a ruby. "That's a roll you'd see on a runway. That's a Christian Dior roll, Steven. They're from this place..." She pivoted on her chair, pointing through the wall. "...four blocks that way. Little green cottage they made a bakery. I'll be back there, tell you what. I might be back there *today*."

"Nothing stopping you."

She pointed her roll at me. "Precisely. And that's what I'm talking about. I can go where I want, even if I was there twenty minutes ago. Which is how things should be, you know?" She watched me, legs crossed, roll poised before her. "Do you know what I mean, Steven?"

"I do," I said. And I did.

She recrossed her legs, holding the roll gingerly, like it could spill. "Because I don't know about you, and the train wrecks you climbed out of. But God, I'm finished with that."

"Me too," I said. Not that things with Amanda were a train wreck—as of two days ago, anyway, they weren't. Just the same, like Nicole, I was finished.

She dimmed an eye. "I mean, I could've dealt with it. What pissed me off was not knowing *why* I dealt with it. When I started with Jeremy, there were reasons. Then it was just..." She pondered the chintzy tabletop. "...stuff. It was just *stuff*, and I was... I don't know. A thing upon the land."

She nodded softly, as if agreeing with her statement. It occurred to me to wonder who Jeremy was, and whether the two of them... well, whether they had anyone else in their life, beyond the two of them. But: Nicole Thorpe sat two feet from me. If I liked, I could climb onto my knees and taste her. And the shine of that knowledge, filling my mind, banished all shadows.

She went on. "It's not even a midlife crisis—I don't want you to think that. My dad had one of those, where suddenly everything needed to be profound. I remember he bought an oboe." She squinted at the air, as if her father's oboe floated there. She shook her head. "This is just... I couldn't in a million years think of something to do that's profound. I just want to take in the scenery."

"You're a thing upon the land," I said.

She studied me. Then she leaned forward, kissing my mouth. Our faces close, she searched my eyes left and right. "You wouldn't know it from hearing me talk, but I'm fucking happy."

I laughed.

"I didn't know happiness could be this *big*," she said.

"I feel good, too."

She patted my cheek. "Go get cleaned up. You look rough."

***

That first morning, we pulled on jackets and drifted through town, no initiative in our step, no destination in mind. We strolled up Florence Avenue, commenting on all that bore comment. An old convertible passed, some Plymouth from the thirties, and we stopped to watch it, autumn trees reflected in its emerald wax. The driver was a glad walrus of a man who touched his cap at us, drove on. I'll be like that someday. I'll be the peaceful stranger. Farther along, on Pine Street, we discovered a yard populated with carved goblins. We browsed among them, bringing our faces to theirs for periods of intense study. They stared past us, like recruits withstanding the scrutiny of drill sergeants. Elsewhere in town, we saw magpies hopping in a driveway. A woman in a brick home combed her drapes with a Hoover attachment. It was a still morning in Sandpoint with sunlight slanting in trees, screw-on sprinkler heads dribbling in lawns.

For lunch, we filled a cooler with beer and sandwiches, and a backpack with blankets and shitty novels, and walked to the beach. It was beautiful out, but being nearly October, the shore was deserted. A gray-haired lady levered a tennis ball for her poodle, but that was all. The bridge into town was likewise deserted, and from the beach we saw in town only a few glinting windshields nosing through intersections. Waves lapped the shore under wheeling, squawking gulls. The far shore was mountains.

After some reading, and tracing fingernails on each other's wrists, Nicole tented her book on her stomach. She asked how I was set for money.

"I have a little," I said, and wondered how little that'd turn out to be. Getting to town yesterday, I'd deposited cash at a local bank, thinking a local account would be harder for Amanda to find. But she had everything else, and likely would have the new account, too, sooner or later. That was fine. I hadn't counted on keeping our money.

Clouds migrated across Nicole's sunglasses. "Well. Add your little to mine, and we have two littles."

"I don't care."

"Bravo!" She lifted her hands, applauding enthusiastically. "That's the correct answer, lover boy. We need what we need to eat, not a dime more. And I guess the house costs money. But hey: if we need money, we'll work." She rolled her face toward me, so that my own face hovered in her lenses. "What would you do, Stevie?"

"For work? Anything."

"Another correct answer. You're really dropping knowledge."

"I don't care what I do."

She stared at the sky. Eventually, she said, "I want to walk dogs."

"You'd be a wet dream of a dog walker."

She laughed. "Yeah?"

"God, yes."

She watched me. I didn't know what she was thinking. Then, leaping to her feet, she jogged down the beach. Returning, she sashayed with her hand before her, an invisible leash pinched in her fingers. She sucked in her cheeks, pouting, tiptoeing as if in heels. Let me just say: you think you're already in love, then the woman you love imitates a slut dog walker. Your heart sublimates into a hot mist. I applauded, wolf-whistling. Nicole strutted past, before strutting back again, hair wild in the breeze. I pulled her down, rolling onto her. I couldn't believe I'd lived so long without coming to this place, with this woman, and feeling this way.

Her hair tangled in the sand, like kelp. I floated in her lenses, framed by sky. "I see you," she said, "at a sidewalk table at a coffee shop. Your legs are crossed."

"What the fuck are you talking about?"

She laughed. "For work! That's your job!"

"I'm drinking coffee?"

"I think so. I'm not sure who's paying you, or what you're doing, but you're *definitely* at a patio table, and *definitely* your legs are crossed." At each "definitely," she thumped my chest.

"Am I wearing a beret?"

"I believe so."

"I could do that."

She thumped my chest. "I *know* you could!"

What I said next, I oughtn't have. I even understood, as my lips formed the words, that I oughtn't be saying them. But things with Nicole felt buoyant, and I don't know, I wanted that buoyancy to keep other things afloat, too. I said, "I actually have a beret somewhere. I was Picasso for Halloween. My kid Knox was my paintbrush. We dressed him up."

A wind kicked up, blowing my hair sideways in Nicole's lenses. Her face behind the lenses was blank, and whatever I'd hoped would float sank fast, taking a lot else down with it. Nicole rolled aside, and sat upright, watched the lake. "Steven," she said. "Fuck you."

"I'm sorry."

"Don't bring them here."

I watched the lake. "I know."

"They're not here. That's why we're here."

Waves hissed the sand.

"I don't want to hear their names, frankly," she said.

"No. I don't either." It was true or not, and either way something in me was decaying.

We sat awhile watching gulls. Nicole glanced in the cooler, then shut the lid without choosing anything.

Our neighbors in Sandpoint were hippies who in another life had taught middle school Civics. They'd strung hammocks in their yard, and painted sunbursts and birds on their house. When Nicole and I returned from dinner one night, they were reclined in their dark yard conversing softly. They were smoking something. I saw only their shadows, but the arm of one shadow lifted and a voice called out. "Greetings!" the man said. "Good evening! Come say hello!"

Nicole laid her purse in the grass, and we stepped over the low fence to their yard. The shadows righted before us, a man and woman distinguishable only by height, as they wore identical long hair and billowy clothing, and as both shadows, standing, jangled with bracelets. "Welcome to you both. To this ground," the man said. He said his name was Ervin.

We followed the couple into their home, which was sweetly fragrant and which—when Ervin hit the lights—revealed itself as a den of glasswares and cushions and cloth slung from the ceiling. Slung from the cloth were strands of patio lights, magentas and violets. The woman, Diane, smoothed a blanket on the futon, inviting us to sit. There was other furniture, but our hosts arranged themselves on the rug at our feet, their legs folded aside like Greek representations. Diane lighted a punk of something. Something latched onto my ankle, and when I looked it was Ervin's hand. "Are you comfortable?" he said. He wore round eyeglasses between his divided gray hair, and I was as comfortable as I could get with another man's fingers encircling my foot. "Yes," I said. "Very much so."

Nicole drew her legs underneath her. "Wow, what a warm home."

Ervin closed his eyes, nodding solemnly. Diane said, "We had this home in our souls a long time. It was locked there. We were in Pico Rivera. You can't live simply in California anymore, the spirit's gone."

"The spirit?" Nicole said.

"We moved there when we were kids. Nineteen?"

"Nineteen," Ervin agreed.

"It was a place..." Diane's gaze dissipated. "...that took you inside of it. You became what it breathed." She touched her throat, smiling dreamily. "There wasn't any friction. Your whole person was in the air."

"That sounds... amazing," Nicole said.

"It's disappeared now. Everyone's in a condominium. There's too much constriction there."

"But we," Ervin covered Diane's hand, "want to hear about your journey. What winds have you sailed?"

It felt good to be asked that question, even if I didn't know how to respond. I thought Nicole would answer, but she only sat with her legs underneath her, a serene expression on her face.

"Maybe," Ervin said, "we should unfold a little." He produced from his clothing what they'd been smoking in the yard, a limp joint he picked with his fingernail before lighting. He asked whether we enjoyed unfolding, and Nicole said she did, she enjoyed it absolutely. She accepted the joint, inhaled. I had some, and for a time the four of us smoked, watching our smoke, not speaking. Ervin pinched the joint out, restored it to his clothing. He said winds of one bearing or another had delivered us to their home, and he was curious which winds they'd been, and what we thought of them.

I didn't quite look at Nicole, and she didn't quite look at me—we looked together at the patch of futon separating us. Not even with each other, in private, were we discussing the winds Ervin referred to. No: we lived together in fresher winds, winds new and alive. But in that kind home, and kind light, smoke curling in our lungs, the lives we'd brought to Sandpoint weren't menacing. We'd detached from all that. We'd relinquished our lives, like a child we'd laid in a crib, late at night. And now Nicole did look at me, and I at her. "Go ahead," I said.

"No." She touched my knee. "You."

I watched Nicole, then faced Ervin and Diane, who waited for me to proceed.

"Well. I had a family in Olympia. A wife and son."

They nodded. It was as if they'd known this already, and I were merely confirming it. It was as if my experience were common to all.

"It got to where," I said, "they weren't part of me anymore. They were one thing, I was something else. I don't know how that happened. I'm not even curious how it happened, really. It did. Then there was life with Nicole, life here." I thought about things. I said, "Truthfully, I don't know much about it. What I'm doing, any of it. But there can be a light, I think. And if you don't turn toward it..." I skated out on a pond of silence.

"We're listening," Diane said.

"Then... there's no light."

The light in the room, at that moment, became a sentient thing. We weren't there. Nothing was. The light lived in its house like a tired, sad giant.

Nicole gazed at me. Diane said, "You're a spirit, Steven. You owe nothing but to love."

***

I'd smoked grass when I was younger, and while smoking interpreted the universe. My college roommate had had to listen to me. I told him there wasn't such thing as food, that food was a construct. Basically, it was chunks of earth we flensed away like blubber from a harpooned whale, then added to our bodies to confiscate Nature's strength. Likewise, there wasn't such thing as Nature. Nor such thing as things. ("Things," I said, rabbit-earing my fingers.) Creation was a single immense ogre of warts, which we divided into separate components so we could pretend there was such thing as time. In the morning after these episodes, I was mortified by what I'd said, and would follow my roommate to breakfast and class, chatting normally—as naturally and normally as I could muster—so as to demonstrate my sanity to him. It became a colossal waste of energy. That's why, eventually, I stopped smoking. But when I awoke the morning after our evening with the neighbors, the Idaho sky was blue in the window, the quilts on our bed were warm, and Nicole's body smooth and warm within them, and I remained convinced of every word I'd uttered. Nicole was a light I'd turned toward. I wouldn't apologize to anyone for that.

The days flew from us, the way Knox liked to cup willow seeds in his hands then open them to the wind. We sipped coffee in the mornings, and walked and read, and one morning in a thick fog we lighted a bonfire on the beach. We plunged into the frigid lake before thrashing ashore, warming ourselves by the flames. A policeman who happened by told us the fire was illegal. We stood before him, shivering like orphans, skin blue. Laughing, he wandered on into the fog. Evenings came, earlier and earlier, and we ate small dinners in the yard before drifting inside to fuck and sleep in each other's sweat. Late in the night, our bodies shaking, we pulled the quilts over our heads, wrestling into a naked knot, believing we'd never be warm again. But heat curled about us. Our muscles slackened. The room paled, the walls and furniture acquiring definition, and soon a blue sky spread in the window. It was day.

It was late October when the phone in our kitchen rang. We hadn't known there was a phone. We were in the yard, watching the aspens and birches that climbed like flames into the firs behind the property. They were gold and orange, and red, and among them stood a willow whose tendrils drooped like the fragments of a detonated thing plummeting to earth. The wind blew, showering leaves like so many coins, and through that hiss we heard the ringing phone. I glanced at Nicole. She went to investigate, and when she didn't return, I followed.

She stood in the kitchen with the phone at her ear, the phone cradle in her hand, and she didn't look happy. I heard the voice on the phone, but not what it said. It went on. Finally Nicole interrupted. "Maybe you could have a life, too. Did you think of that?" she said.

The voice exploded. Nicole held the phone away before saying into the mouthpiece, "You know what, forget it. Here." She dumped everything in my arms, and left the room with hands raised.

A moment passed, the phone waiting. I sat. "Hi," I said.

"You're fucking disgusting," Amanda said.

She was a tide of flames, only I wasn't flammable.

"Making me talk to that cunt? Seriously?"

"What's this about?" I said.

"She's real sweet, by the way. Bet she has a spotless bill of health. What's this *about*? Is that what you said?"

"Do you have something to say?"

"It's about you fucking that cunt, Steven."

"Don't talk like that. I won't listen to it."

"Christ," she said.

"If you have something to say, say it. I'll hear you out."

"Is that really your tack here? The high road?"

"You called me, Amanda."

"Don't 'Amanda' me. Fuck you."

I was silent.

"What do you have to say, Steven? That's the point here."

"I don't have anything to say. I'm happy."

"Oh Jesus. Jesus, Jesus."

"I hope you can be happy, too."

"Well, that's not something I worry about. I'm a bit too adult for that, Steven. You know who I hope can be happy is your son. I'll go ahead and get him on the line, actually." Her voice left the phone. "Knox?" she called. "Knox, honey, can you come in here? Your daddy wants to talk to you. He wants to tell you where he's been." Then she was back with me. "Good luck with this, Steven. Try not to fuck him up too bad."

Something tightened in my chest, like when I was in school and was called on to read aloud. I breathed. I thought: I'm a human being with joy in my life. I live in joy. I'm a thing upon the land.

"Daddy?" Knox said.

"Hi, son!" I croaked.

He asked where I was.

"Son, well I'm somewhere else now."

"Where?"

"I've gone to live somewhere else. It's somewhere that makes me happy."

He didn't speak.

"Son?"

"Okay, Daddy," he said.

"Hey." I sat forward on the chair. "No, hey. Knox, are you there? Are you listening?"

He waited.

"This is a good thing, okay? I don't want you being sad about this. I know it feels sad, because we're not together, but son everyone gets a life. Okay, it's a gift. Life is a gift. I have one, just like you have one. Like your mom has one. And we have to try to be happy. Are you listening to me, Knox? You have to go where happiness is. That's all you can do. Now you might be mad at your dad. Are you mad at me, Knox? It's all right if you are. But you'll be a grownup soon. And there might be somewhere you need to go to be happy. And I hope you remember your dad, Knox. Don't be afraid, okay?"

"Okay," he said.

"I'm going now. I want you to be happy, son. Don't forget what your dad told you."

He hung up first. I placed the phone on the cradle and watched it there.

I was still in the kitchen when Nicole appeared in the doorway. The phone was in my lap. "I'm sorry about that," I said.

She leaned against the doorjamb, arms folded. "How'd she get this number?"

"I don't know."

"Don't you have a phone she can call?"

"I wasn't answering."

She scrutinized me awhile.

"Sorry," I said again.

"Steven, I don't like her in this house. Not her voice, not anything."

"I know. I don't, either."

"You don't understand. She can't be here."

I gestured vaguely. "I don't know what I could've done, Nic."

"It's not your fault. I'm not saying that. I'm saying: if that woman's here, then all this..." She stirred her finger at the house. "...isn't what it needs to be. Do you get that?"

"Yeah."

"It doesn't matter whose fault it is."

I stared at the phone. Then, wrapping the cord around my fist, I jerked it from the wall. The jack dislodged, taking some plaster with it. Nicole went out in the yard.

That weekend, I bought a dress from a boutique in town and laid it out for Nicole on our bed. It was plum-colored, strappy and lean, and despite Amanda's call, the dress wasn't purchased as an apology. It was to prove apologies of any kind, to anyone, weren't warranted.

Against the quilts on the bed, the dress wasn't as alluring as I'd hoped. Some of the quilt patches were themselves plum-colored, or once had been, and lying upon them the dress resembled a dye that'd leached from the quilt and pooled there. I stripped the quilts, arranging the dress on the sheet underneath, but then it resembled an undergarment discovered in the bed while turning it down. I breathed, calming myself. I hunted through the linen closet in the hall, where I unearthed a cream-colored duvet that'd once been white, perhaps. I made up the bed with that, and found that by switching on only one dim lamp, the duvet's discolorations were muted. I laid the dress on the bed, and stood awhile in the tableau I'd composed, tapping my lips, senses alert for other discordance. Some aromatic was in order, but I'd made it no farther than the kitchen, where I thought I'd seen candles, when the back door opened, and Nicole was home.

I wished immediately I'd doctored up the whole house, and not just one room. I didn't like Nicole knocking around in the kind of ordinary lighting you'd find in any house, in any city, when this was our house together, on Florence Avenue in Sandpoint. She'd been hiking that afternoon, and wore a down vest, earmuffs. She pried off the earmuffs, eyeing me strangely. "What's with you?" she said.

"I'll show you."

In the bedroom, she plucked off her mittens and stalked about the dress like a sniffing wolf. Finally she held the dress against herself, and peered out at me through the hair that fell over her eyes.

"Put it on," I said.

"This makes me want to fuck."

I laughed. "Maybe that's the idea. Put it on."

She laid the dress on the bed, and shooed me out.

"I want to stay."

"Go," she said.

She shut the door, and while she changed I stood in the dark hall, trying to feel the two of us at the end not just of a hall, but of a narrow passage leading out from everything else. Everyone else. A person would have to travel a great distance to reach Nicole and me, and if we heard someone coming we'd simply flee deeper into the passage, and deeper still, never to be found.

The door opened, and there was Nicole in the plum dress, one smooth leg placed ahead of the other. The fabric lay delicately upon her, as if a breeze would carry it off, leaving her bare. Behind her in the room was a candle she'd found, its lick of flame wavering on the dresser. "Are we fucking now," she said, "or what?"

I closed the door behind us, and before touching Nicole I admired her posture in the room. "How does it feel?"

"Like you're watching me."

"You look... otherworldly."

Eyes locked on mine, she pushed a strap off her shoulder.

"Is this how you want to feel? How you feel right now?" I said.

"I'll feel pretty good in a minute."

"Feel this moment, Nic. This is what we have."

She put a finger to my lips.

We drove to Coeur d'Alene, and took a dinner cruise down the lake. It was an enchanted evening. The boat was a fine barge, something like a riverboat, with festive lights the size of pears strung along the deck. October had become November, the tourists vanishing; our boat's capacity was a hundred or more, but with the exception of an elderly couple huddled on the viewing deck, and a lone bachelor at the bar, we were the only souls aboard. We followed the lower deck to a place near the prow, where we leaned over the bulwark, watching the black water churn by, flecked with white where the hull chopped waves. The shore was pure wilderness: deep timber and rocky glades gliding by in the moonlight. But my eyes adjusted, and I glimpsed in the timber the procession of darkened homes there, all shuttered for the season. Seeing that, I knew we were sailing through a deeper, more formidable species of night.

"I want to swim," Nicole said. She leaned out over the bulwark, lifting to her toes. I thought that might be it, she might slip in and drown. She seesawed back. "Christ, I feel light, Steven. I'm just *air*."

We stayed at the resort in town, its corridors deserted. Strolling the boardwalk that night, we gazed up at the hotel's twenty stories of darkened windows, near the top of which floated the single lighted pane that was ours. The room was an extravagant expense. That was concerning now that Amanda knew where I was, and could maybe get our money, and now that I'd paid months of rent, and money was low. But I couldn't imagine what money was for if not this, and so the following week I brought Nicole to Canada, to a hot springs there. In a cedar-walled room with portraits of snowy peaks, we drank as lavish a Bordeaux as can be purchased in Invermere, British Columbia, then scampered across the grounds to the smoking pools. When the steam cleared, we saw actual snowy peaks reaching into the stars. A couple from Calgary, who'd been at the hot springs several weeks, said the snow was advancing rapidly. When they'd arrived, the peaks were bare.

That Canadian snow ran down those mountains, filling that Canadian valley, then migrated south until the day, late in November, the first flakes of it whirled in Sandpoint. I was at the filling station near the bridge, perusing magazines. The door chimed opened and closed, admitting winter chill, while at the end of the counter a single hot dog glistened under sweaty heat lamps. "Yeah, I think it's starting," someone said, and looking up from *Western Lifestyles Magazine*, I saw through the window the snow blowing and pirouetting like a hatch of flies. It was midafternoon, but already leaden with dusk, and I had the feeling, watching that snow, that something had slipped through my hands, the way if you grip sand too tightly it pours away. I was across the street, hurrying through the neighborhood, before I noticed *Western Lifestyles Magazine* was still in my hand. I dropped it in a yard, which was already accumulating snow, and kept on.

When I reached the house, Nicole wasn't anywhere, and I panicked. A grim knowledge polluted my breathing. "Nic?" I said, racing through the rooms. "Nic?" My voice in that house was hoarse and pathetic. I leaned on a chair in the kitchen, steadying myself, thinking I might pass out. Through the sliding door, finally, I saw Nicole on the patio, watching the snow fall.

Joining her, I closed the door softly behind me. She sat in an Adirondack chair, legs crossed, hands in pockets. Without looking at me, she said: "Sit down, Steven. It's gorgeous out here."

I sat in the other chair. Ervin and Diane's door opened, and they walked into their yard, lifting faces to the sky.

"Nic," I said eventually, "are you happy?"

"Mm?" She watched the snow.

"I need to know you're happy."

"What're you talking about?"

I slid toward her on my chair. Before I could speak, she laid a hand on my arm. "Steven, calm down. I'm happy."

Snow dusted her hair and lashes. She tilted her head to catch flakes on her tongue.

"Because..." I said, "... I'd do anything."

"I know that."

"This kind of thing doesn't happen to everyone."

"Can we," she said, "watch the snow?"

The house when I woke seemed muted, as if padded with cotton; I went in the living room, and parting the curtains discovered a blinding universe of white, the drifts piled over cars, mailboxes, mounting clear to the windowsill at my waist. Across the street, a neighbor I hadn't met flung shovel loads off his walk. A plow passed, its volley of snow further interring the neighborhood's vehicles. It was a day to sip cocoa in pajamas, yielding the town to municipal authorities. But holding still seemed like a dangerous proposition. The moment I paused, everything might catch me.

Returning to the bedroom, I tore open the curtains, flooding the air with light. Nicole groaned, yanking the duvet over her head, but I yanked it from her hands, the duvet and sheets both, and threw everything on the floor. "Steven, what the *fuck*?" She curled like a pill bug, trying to hug herself to sleep.

"It's incredible out there. Let's do something."

"*What?*"

"Let's go."

"Fuck," she said, "what time is it?"

"I don't know what time it is. I'm not a clock."

For a man with no ideas, I sure was avid to get moving. Things were getting manic, which would've alarmed someone in better possession of his faculties, but which to me was immaterial. Because: fuck my faculties. I wanted *Nicole.*

Dressed in our snow gear, such as it was (neither of us owned better than jeans), I led Nicole across the yard, our legs burying like pegs. Reaching the mailbox, I saw her floundering and trudged back to help. I got her out to the street, and batted snow from her thighs and rear. It wouldn't come off her jeans. I batted more, until she swatted away my hand. "Let's just fucking go," she said.

I stood back from her. Nicole lifted and dropped her hands.

"Do you not want to go?" I said. "We can stay."

She glanced at the yard, which would be as treacherous to cross a second time as it had been the first.

"Let's stay," I said.

"No, goddamn it, just walk." She flung her hand at the street. "*Walk.*"

Nicole would be happy, I decided, once the morning gave her cause to be. I kissed her cheek and set out ahead of her, bouncing in my boots. I *was* happiness. I exuded it. My happiness would shine upon this woman, this creature, and warm her like a summer's day.

It was a gorgeous morning, achingly gorgeous, with shadows mapped on the snow and no vehicles in the street besides occasional trucks and four-wheelers trailing dervishes of exhaust. We reached downtown, the snow on Nicole's jeans now thawed to a damp slop. I'd hoped for food, but not a restaurant in sight was open. That was fine. We'd power through that. On the other side of that, we'd find joy.

"Can we just get coffee?" Nicole said, the coffee shop being the only open business on First Avenue.

"I thought we'd get breakfast."

Her shoulders slumped. "I'm fucking cold, Steven. I want coffee."

"There'll be coffee at breakfast. You'll be glad we kept going."

"Kept *going*? Where are we *going*?"

Taking her mittened hand, I led her up the street. "We'll find a place. It'll be perfect."

We didn't. And it wasn't. All we found, actually, was the Yoke's Market where we'd rendezvoused months earlier, and all we found there was stale donuts a stock boy in an apron was dropping in a sack.

"I'll actually take a few of those," I said.

Nicole gazed up the aisle.

"These?" the boy said. "These are trash."

"Just sell us some."

"I can't vend this shit. Dude, this is garbage."

We bought bananas and Hostess snacks and found by the deli some tepid coffee in urns. "This is still fun," I said, but we were miles from the house and Nicole's jeans and boots were soaked; she had nothing to say. We wound up throwing away the food and coffee. No mention was made of our being at Yoke's Market off Highway 2 in Sandpoint, Idaho, which I'd once thought would be a meaningful location for us, for our story.

Nicole was bedridden for a week, vomiting and shivering and bundling in the duvet and quilts like a morphing caterpillar. Outside, the snow melted. The yard became a muddy swamp, rank odors wafting up from the flooded crawlspace. Once she was well, Nicole's phone started ringing. The first calls were in broad daylight—"Hello?" she'd say, carrying her phone up the hall, conversation trailing off behind her. But soon her phone rang at night, too. Climbing from bed, she'd usher the glowing screen into another room, a holy candle. I'd hear her say, "Well hello, you. What do you think I'm doing? It's two in the morning..."

Her phone rang one night in particular. She carried it into the kitchen, and after counting to sixty I threw off the sheets and followed her. She sat by the window, moonlight bathing her face and the only sound in the room the thin voice in her ear. "That's true," she whispered to the voice.

"Who is it?" I said.

Nicole started violently, chair legs scraping linoleum. "Christ," she said, resting her forehead in her hand, catching her breath.

"Tell me who it is. Who's next?"

To the phone she said, "I'll call you back."

Crossing the room, I confiscated her phone and smashed it on the table. The screen popped, glass sprinkling the floor.

"Oh, there you go," she said. "Now you're a problem solver."

"You fucking skank."

"Get it out of your system, Steven. Show us how powerful you are."

Her phone was broken enough, but I threw it anyway. The glass sliding door, where I'd aimed, splintered into moonlit cracks.

"You're resolving this beautifully," she said.

I dropped in a chair.

"You're fucking pathetic," she said.

The weather the next morning was slate-colored, lifeless. I awoke on the sofa without full understanding of what'd brought me there, and without blankets. The furniture around me—each item of it—wallowed in a bath of dull light. No shadows. Or else everything in shadow. It looked like furniture a family had left behind. It looked, I found myself thinking, like the furniture that'd be in those homes I'd seen on our cruise, those vacant homes in the trees.

Nicole walked past, carrying an armload of sweaters. I closed my eyes, swimming upstream toward a moment that wasn't this one. But this moment carried forward, carrying me with it. Through the window, I saw Nicole stuff her sweaters into the Nissan. When she returned, I said: "Would you slow down, please? Think about this."

"Have you seen my sunglasses?"

"Just relax, Nic. Let's talk."

Her car was loaded before I pulled on my jeans. I trotted after her out of the house, buckling my belt, skidding barefoot in the grass. "Nic, listen to me..."

She tossed her purse in the backseat.

"Let's keep trying this," I said.

It was this remark that caught her attention. The car door stopped in her hand, half ajar. "What'd you say?"

"I'm not done with us. Let's keep trying."

She laughed.

"I mean it."

"Steven, I don't know how to break this to you. We never were trying. I thought you got that."

"I want to try."

"And I," she said, "don't."

There should've been more. She should've embraced me, or plucked a mitten from her hand, patted my cheek. Instead, the Nissan drove away. A door banged open, and Ervin crossed his lawn to speak with me, but I jumped in my own car to chase her. She wasn't gone. She was at the park around the corner, or at the bakery. She was at the bookshop or coffee shop or beach. But when I reached the beach, it was just me there. I didn't even see the lady with her poodle.

Walking down to the water, I saw a car that wasn't Nicole's sail out onto the bridge, getting smaller and smaller. It vanished from sight half-way across. Nicole, I decided, could be recovered. And if I couldn't have her, I'd have someone else. And if I couldn't have that woman, I'd have another. There'd be someone in my life. I wouldn't have just this lake with sky mirrored in it. I wouldn't have just these waves, licking away the sand.

A Kind of Person

2004

Mindy'd been in Josh's math class freshman year, and ignorant as Josh was, I can't imagine how ignorant Mindy, a junior at the time, must've been. If I recall, theirs was one of those math classes that was held in a "positive thinking" room, with bright colors and motivational posters and reduced distraction and nine or ten academic staff on hand at all times, helping the students carry out long division in a manner respectful of their individual limitations, which in that room were called "opportunities." Seventeen years old, Mindy was, counting on her damn fingers.

To be honest, I can't quite place her. She was one of the blondes who wore makeup and sequined jeans, or else was one of the brunettes whose jeans had sequins in them and who liked wearing makeup. Concerning the female population at Edwall High School, you could pretty much let any one individual stand for the whole. Which was as true for the males, I suppose. Anyways, whoever Mindy was, I can picture her and Josh studying math together in that jolly room. They're kneeling on the floor, sorting out wooden blocks. They get all the green ones in a stack, they get a 70-minute break and a box of apple juice.

The only reason we were thinking about Mindy that afternoon is Josh was obligating us to think about her. We were on the porch of the ranch house Tyler's family used during harvest, just enjoying some beers and chew. Tyler and I, for our own parts, would've been content to leave things at beers and chew, and leave the conversation where we usually left it, which was on the subject of how we might comport ourselves with this or that set of breasts, given the opportunity. That was good conversation for a May afternoon. But Josh, he wanted to talk about Mindy Barnes. "Old Mindy Barnes," he kept calling her. According to his best information, this girl had moved to Spokane to explore her talents as a prostitute.

Josh had been briefing us on the Mindy situation for ten minutes or longer, during which interval Tyler'd been shaking his head steadily. When Josh finally paused for breath, Tyler said, "You know what, Joshua Simon?" He tapped his head. "You need to shut the fuck up when you get something in your cranium you think is true."

"Excuse me?" Josh said, squinting at Tyler. "Ex*cuse* me?"

Tyler pinched out some Cope. "Fucking streetwalkers, fucking women of the night. I don't know how to tell you this, old buddy. But your life has no connection to all that sexy dangerous shit. You're a corn-fed fucking moron from Edwall, Washington, just like everybody else."

"I don't know what you're talking about, Tyler," Josh said. "Mindy Barnes is a hooker. It's a goddamn fact of Creation."

Tyler tucked the chew in his lip, dusted his hand on his jeans. "Nope."

Josh sat taller on the bucket he was sitting on. "It's true, goddamn it! She needed to make money for her kid or something. She had a drug dependency or something like that."

"You just want to be that kind of guy knows hookers," Tyler said. "It's fucking embarrassing, honestly."

"Kind of guy knows hookers," Josh muttered. "Knowing hookers ain't a kind of guy, Tyler."

"It sure is. Boy and your eyes light up when you think it might be you."

It was a warm spring day under empty skies, and from the Copelands' porch we could see out over the fields to the silo and trees marking the Uptons' farm. We could see north almost to Canada and south almost to Oregon, and crickets were sawing like they usually did only later in the year. The Copelands' porch was our preferred location for afternoons like this. We couldn't get into the house, of course—everyone lived in town during the year and kept their farm places shuttered—but from where we sat we could see miles up the road, and if someone came looking for us we'd have time to finish our beers and maybe another beer, and tuck the bottles in the box and bury the box and brush our teeth before anyone got close enough to see what we were doing. Every so often, one of us pissed off the porch into the sunshine. That's what I was doing now.

"What's your opinion, Michael James?" Tyler said.

I zipped up. "Knowing hookers is a kind of person," I said. "No doubt about it."

"Oh..." Josh waved his hand. "...what the fuck would he know?"

"Probably he'd know more than us," Tyler said. "Probably he's read all the literature."

"Shit." Josh spat on the porch.

"I bet he's studied hooker life cycles. Hooker mating procedures."

"This fat tub of shit ain't even touched a standard pussy," Josh said, "let alone the industrial model. And it's not like hooker mating procedures is any secret, Tyler."

I walked back and sat at their feet, my shoulders against one of the porch posts. Dumb as he was, Josh was right about what he'd said. I'd never touched a girl. In fact, the idea of touching a girl was so alien to me that I partially suspected no one touched girls, not really. I thought maybe they were only for wishing you could touch them, like rainbows. You get to be a fat fuck like I was, you believe peculiar things.

"Well," Josh said, easing back against the house, "It's a true fact about Mindy Barnes. I wish for your all's ignorant sakes it wasn't, but it is. You can ask Merle Dobbs about it. He saw Mindy at the bus station down there, all splattered with makeup and all. Skanky little dress on."

"Man," Tyler said. "Merle thinks everyone turns tricks."

Josh went on. "He said he saw a john grab her muff, even. I don't know how you make something like that up. Listen, boys, I ain't selling you any bill of goods here. Old Mindy, she's taken to the ancient trade. Sleeping by day and by night trafficking her comforts." He looked at Tyler, then at me. He gazed over the fields in what happened to be the direction of Spokane, the roof's long shadow indicating it like an arrow. He said, "And boy, that little thing. She'd be tickled to see me."

We were silent. Tyler looked at Josh. "What'd you just say?"

"I mean if I were to appear in her life," Josh said. "She'd feel rescued, I bet. Boy and she wouldn't be mistaken, neither. I'd do right by her."

"Brother, you say so much ignorant shit so fast I don't know what to shoot down first. She'd feel *rescued*?"

"Oh, Tyler, she liked me. Math confused her something terrible, so we just passed the time. We had that..." Josh snapped his fingers. "...what people get between them. Biology."

"It's chemistry, you stupid fucking elephant, and no you didn't have it."

"She used to look at me? Boy, you wouldn't think hookers got by on their eyes, but *whew*. It was this whole highway of meaning flowing between us."

"Brother, you scare me."

"I don't mean 'meaning' in some creepy way."

"Well, yes you do. But that's not why you're scary."

Josh shook his head. "You're talking some bullshit, amigo. Scary? Name one good reason I'm scary."

"You just could never understand."

"Whatever that means," Josh said. I didn't say anything, but knew what Tyler meant.

"Well," Josh said, nodding at where the house shadow pointed. "I'm doing it."

"Doing...?"

"Life's there for the picking, boys. I won't stand idly by."

"Please tell me this has nothing to do with hookers."

Josh pushed to his feet. "I'm finding that girl."

"Lord."

"You coming with me?"

Tyler shook his head. He jetted some spit off the porch. Though eventually Tyler pushed to his feet. "Yeah, I'll come with you. Fucking asshole." And if Tyler was going, I was, too.

***

Spokane was an hour off, and driving there we got loaded off some Grand-Dad whiskey we stole from Josh's house. It was his mom's bourbon—his mom who wouldn't miss it. She was drunk herself, and if it happened she broke the surface of sobriety for a breath or two before sounding again, like the great whale she was, she'd just assume she herself was the culprit in the case of the missing Grand-Dad. It was simple theft, getting that whiskey from Ms. Hall. Maybe Josh wished it wasn't so easy to fool his mom, but I didn't—and still don't—credit Joshua Simon Hall with a very complex interior life. Mostly, I think, he liked getting fucked up and doing as he pleased.

We rode in Tyler's dad's truck, Tyler and Josh in the front seat and me in the extended cab, which is where a fat fuck always ends up, counterintuitive as that is. Air thundered through the windows. Mr. Copeland's David Allan Coe played loud on the stereo, that old jerky stick yelling on about thirteen kids and dogs, and houses of chickens and hogs. Joshua, God forgive him, yelled right through the music about how events between him and Mindy would unfold. Best I could tell, his plan was to inform Mindy that her living days didn't have to be the tragedy she'd made of them. She had value as a human being and mother. By Josh's reckoning, expressing these sentiments would make Mindy fall in his arms and weep, at which juncture he'd stuff himself inside of her. Watching Tyler's eyes in the rearview, I knew what he thought of Josh's plans. Of course I thought the same. But we were headed to Spokane—to where the hookers were in Spokane, no less—and admittedly I myself hoped sex'd be in the air. Maybe we'd find Mindy Barnes, maybe we wouldn't. But that sex would be floating around, and with luck I could catch some of it, like coming down with a cold.

Eastern Washington is all distance, wheat and sky, but nearing Spokane the pine forests closed over us. We lost an hour of daylight in thirty seconds. Then there it was: the little city that for some country mice from Edwall might just as well have been Shanghai. It lay in its valley, lights shimmering. Even Josh fell silent. There was a great deal that could happen in Spokane. Certainly everything we wished for could happen, and much else.

We ate burgers at Dick's Restaurant, which was where we ate when we came to town with our folks. From our picnic table at Dick's, we saw interstate traffic racing by on the overpass, and bums under the overpass, digging through trash barrels and weeds. Now and again, we added some Grand-Dad to our cups of Pepsi. Meanwhile, Josh read a map he'd found in Mr. Copeland's glove box. He thought it'd hold some clues as to the whereabouts of Spokane's pussy-for-hire industry.

Tyler nodded at Josh. "What're you finding there, pardner?"

Josh lifted the map, glancing from the page to the street and back again, as if what he held were a photograph of the world, and not merely a description. "What's that, Fourth Avenue?"

"Third," Tyler said. "And they ain't 'avenues,' they're 'streets.'"

Josh frowned at the map, then turned it upside down. "Oh shit, okay." He folded the thing closed, or tried to. "We're just around the corner from it."

"From . . . ?"

Josh smashed the map as closed as he could get it, then pushed it away from him. He jutted his chin at the darkness hanging over the city. "From all that twat, fool. It's just up yonder."

Tyler watched Josh awhile, then placed his hamburger, carefully, in its basket. "Joshua. Can you tell us again what exactly you aim to do? I know you're hoping to find Mindy Barnes and all. I know you want to baptize her into your church. But let me get this straight. There's going to be some hooker walking the street somewhere. And you're going to holler out to her, 'Excuse me, ma'am, can you direct me to Mindy Barnes from Edwall Senior High?' This is your goddamn plan?"

"Well. It could be she *is* Mindy."

Tyler stared at Josh. His face was like one of those stone heads on that tropical island.

"Hey." Josh raised his hands. "Anything could happen. I live under a lucky star."

"You live under a goddamn retarded brain, Joshua. You are a victim of mental retardation. The first piece of tail you see walking the goddamn sidewalk? You think that'll be the sole individual in this city you're hoping to find? I can't..." Tyler gestured at his own mouth, like someone who'd eaten a pepper.

"Now just calm down a minute," Josh said.

"...I can't form with words the degree of your fucking idiocy."

"All we have tonight is a fact-finding mission. Just think about it like that. Maybe we find Mindy? Maybe we don't? We're assembling information, Tyler. It'll lead somewhere promising. I'm confident."

Tyler returned to his burger. "Trust me, Joshua," he said through his chewing. "You *not* having confidence isn't the particular problem we're plagued with today."

"Give me that fucking Grand-Dad," Josh said, reaching for it. "Come on, give it here. This is the goddamn time of our lives."

Despite Josh's research, there weren't hookers to be found around the corner from Dick's Restaurant. Instead, Sprague Avenue through downtown was an ordinary street. It had galleries on it and places with mannequins in the windows and banks. Josh cast his gaze around, left and right, but nowhere he looked was there any pussy for sale. It pissed him off. Finally an ordinary woman passed, just a lady in cargo pants and a hoodie, and Josh reached across Tyler to pound the truck's horn.

"Jesus." Tyler shoved him away. "The fuck was that?"

Hearing the horn, the woman leapt back and watched us, frightened.

"I thought that could be one."

"Jesus Lord, do you think every..." Tyler interrupted himself. "Nope. Nope, I can't do it. I won't enter that mind of yours."

"Fucking stop the truck. I'll get us directions."

"Directions?" Tyler's eyebrows climbed clear to his hair. "*Directions?*"

"Look for a nigger or somebody. Somebody's got to know where these fillies operate."

"And just like that? That's how you'll pose the question? 'Uh, excuse me, sir, can you tell us how to get into some pussy around here?'"

"Tyler..." Josh shook his head. "...you know, you're getting difficult to be around. You don't understand a damn thing."

"*I* don't understand? *I* don't...Josh, you tie peoples' brains in fucking knots with the shit you think and say. You got that stupidity just *para*lyzes folks."

"Criminal trades," Josh pinched the air delicately, "you've got to put the matter subtly. You've got to know what to *say*, so the other party knows what to say *back*. That way information flows without anybody incrimnifying himself."

Tyler'd checked out. There was only so much Joshua Hall a person could admit into his ears at one go, if he wished to keep his bearing on the world. Meanwhile, Josh waited for Tyler to pull over. When he didn't, I guess old boy decided he couldn't afford that subtlety he'd talked about earlier. At a stoplight, he leaned his head out the window to shout at a bum: "Hey, old timer! Where's a guy go in these parts to get his tip sucked?"

Tyler burned through the intersection, smashing Josh's ear on the door. But the bum must've said something. "Back there!" Josh hollered, cupping his ear. "Guy said back the other way! Motherfucker, turn around!"

Little or not, Spokane is a city and it was Friday; there were women around, dressed like women sometimes dress. Discerning what was a hooker from what wasn't proved more difficult than anticipated. We were east of downtown, where everything was warehouses and switchyards and weeds. It was where you found hookers, but anywhere we saw onc girl we saw others with her, and usually at least one in the pack certainly wasn't a whore. When we did see a lone girl, usually there was a fella nearby. Maybe that man was her john, but maybe he was just a fella taking his girl out on Friday, and even Joshua Simon Hall knew you didn't tug a guy's sleeve, asking if you could chat up his hooker later, once he was finished.

We drove clear down Sprague, nearly to Idaho, then came back that same way, peering in parking lots and under streetlamps. We still were drinking (Tyler looked old enough to buy us Olde English) and Josh still was talking. According to his new idea, Mindy'd offer him a free fuck just the moment she saw him, before he spoke a word, on account of her joy at seeing his face. Afterwards, or maybe after a second fuck, they'd discuss her liberation. Probably, Josh explained, she'd never be a respectable woman. But they could find her a clean apartment and a job with nice pay, and excepting all the free fucks she'd keep giving him, whenever he wanted one, she'd develop a degree of moral rectitude. This'd be good for everyone, her kid included. Especially it'd be good for Josh. "Woo-ee!" he said, twisting the cap onto his malt drink. "Boys, there are fine days in my future!"

The first girl all of us agreed was a hooker stood on the curb near a Vietnamese restaurant, her blonde hair piled everywhere and her pink shirt the size of a dinner bib. There was that shirt, a skirt and boots, and everything else was tummy and legs. Anyone could see what she was. She watched us cruise by, and I can't imagine how we looked to that girl: three country faces hovering like moons in the cab of an F-350.

Up a ways, Tyler pulled into a pawn shop with barred windows and a flashing electric sign. The parking lot was empty. "Well," he asked Josh, "is that Mindy Barnes, or should I keep driving?"

Josh peered in the rearview, as if he could see the girl back there.

"At your word, captain," Tyler said.

Josh swallowed his spit. "All right. Let's do it."

"You sure, cub scout? You don't seem so full of vinegar."

Josh pushed at the wheel. "Go."

Easing into the road, Tyler drove us back to the Vietnamese place; the hooker slid into view, standing in the light falling out from the diner. I'd never eaten Vietnamese food, and if this place was the standard I never would. It looked like a laundromat in there. Tyler pulled into the parking lot. The girl approached us, walking funny in her heels. Lowering his window, Tyler said: "Not me, darling. It's this love-struck gorilla sitting next to me."

He meant she should walk around to the other window, but the girl climbed onto the running board, leaning in over Tyler's lap. The wind blew her hair. She tucked it behind her ear, looking at Josh, then at me, then at Tyler. Chewing her gum, she said, "What's this, the dick taxi?" She couldn't have been even our age. She looked like someone's kid sister.

"My friend wants to ask you something," Tyler said.

"Which one? Fat ass?"

Tyler nodded at Josh. "That one."

The girl, Tyler and myself all waited for Josh to speak. "Um," he said, fidgeting and rubbing his legs. I assumed he'd ask something about Mindy Barnes, and where she was, but it turned out we were finished with Mindy for the night. In fact, in all the years following that night, I never heard Josh say Mindy's name again.

"So," Josh said. "Well, how're you doing tonight?"

She waited for him to go on, then lost interest and said to the three of us generally, "You know you boys are the freshest faces I've ever seen down here. Look at your faces."

We were silent.

"It's a nice change. God, we get some trolls." She rested her elbow on the door, her cheek on her palm, looking dreamy and bored. Her eyes studied us, then went to the bottle between Tyler's legs. Lifting it out, she drank a belt of it, hair blowing again. She smacked her lips. "So you boys go to Ferris, or what?"

Tyler said we didn't.

"I didn't think so. You're too charming for Ferris."

Past Josh's ear, in the shadows near the restaurant, I noticed a man sitting at a picnic table. As I watched, he stood and came into the light. He looked strange, with his leather jacket and with the blunt sort of face Russians have in movies. The girl noticed him, and leaning into the truck, said, "Hey, listen. One of you has to pay, but if you do there's somewhere we can go. Everyone'll get some, I swear. My friends are easy."

The man crossed the parking lot.

"But you got to pay," she said, stepping off the truck and strolling away.

The man knuckled Josh's window. After a second, he lowered it.

"Howdy, gentlemen," the man said. Besides his hair, which stood straight up, his features all were saggy—his eyelids, ears, all of it, like weights hung off his face. I didn't think he'd said "howdy" before in his life. The word didn't fit his mouth. When none of us spoke, he said, "You are satisfied? She is . . . ?" He twirled his hand.

"We'll take her," Josh said. He'd found his tongue finally.

The man nodded. "Very good. Two hundred."

"Two *hun*dred?"

"Josh . . ." Tyler warned, but Josh wasn't the sort to heed warnings. He said, "Two hundred for *that*? What's she, a damn figure skater?"

"One hundred per," the man said. "Third, I throw in free. Let's go."

"Oh, sir you're mistaken. These boys . . ." Josh hiked his thumb at Tyler and me. "Why, they're just observers. They're harmless virgins."

"One-fifty." The man snapped his fingers. "Pay me."

Josh considered the offer, but I wished he'd consider it faster. The man was nervous, glancing over his shoulder, and if his nerves got too jumpy I wanted to be somewhere else. "Shit," Josh said finally, digging out his wallet.

"Hurry up," the man said.

Josh counted his bills, then counted a second time. He glanced at Tyler. "I got seventy."

Quick as that, the man left the truck, whistling for his girl to follow. Without a glance our direction, she clicked her heels after him. "Now hold on!" Josh shouted. "We're getting it, hold on!"

The man stopped, looked at us, and walked back fast. Josh told Tyler to hurry. "Come on, we need eighty bucks."

"You fucking dickhead. I don't have eighty bucks!"

"What?"

Tyler lowered his voice. "I don't have ten bucks. I bought gas."

The man reached us. "Where is it?" He held out his hand. "Give it to me."

"Well." Josh chuckled. "It seems my friend . . ."

I handed the money over his shoulder. No one did anything, then Josh added my bills to his and paid up. The man counted, and folded the money into his pocket. "Two hours," he said, showing us two fingers. He stepped away, and the girl came toward us.

Her name, or leastways the name she gave us, was Kris, and riding in the back with me she might've been any of the girls Tyler and Josh brought around on weekends, girls I knew from tagging along. The only difference between Kris and Edwall girls was Kris's skimpy clothing and overabundant perfume (though we knew girls like that, too). The other difference was we'd paid Kris, which I'd hoped would give me the feeling I could do to her as I pleased, but which hadn't yet.

Where Kris brought us was a blue duplex in a poor part of town, on a street without streetlights. Our cowboy music blared out the windows, and we were drinking in the cab and shouting, but when Tyler killed the engine, we stepped into a night of pure silence. There only was dogs barking somewhere. The duplex's lawn was dirt, with kids' toys scattered through it. Just one of the building's windows was lighted.

Kris'd called ahead, and when we went in, the two friends she'd mentioned waved from the sofa. They were sharing a pipe back and forth, and I remember thinking the pipe's contents could've been anything in the world—any of the chemicals I'd heard about in music and movies, or even something truly beyond my knowing. They weren't much to see, these friends of Kris's. They wore sweats and t-shirts, and beer cans and cardboard pizza sheets lay everywhere around them. But they were girls, sure enough. Josh and Tyler dropped down next to them, Josh on the sofa, Tyler in an armchair. Kris went upstairs to change.

The four of them talked awhile before the fatter girl, the brunette, glanced at me, then glanced at me again. I was drunk, but there's a kind of drunk where shyness is worse, and I'd kept myself near the door. "You can sit down with us, you know," the girl said.

"Yeah," Josh said. "Sit down, Michael, Jesus. Don't lurk over there."

The girl moved over. I sat with her.

"Mikey's what you'd call the cerebellum type," Josh said.

"Cerebral," Tyler said, but Josh paid him no mind.

The girl who'd asked me to sit, besides her chubby face had a greasy ponytail, and just in how she looked at me I saw her weighing pros and cons. She was trying to figure if there was upside to me. I wanted to tell her not to bother. Better not to get pussy, I thought, than be what some girl in a shitty duplex talked herself into. But also, I admit, I hoped it'd work. I hoped she'd talk herself into me.

Kris joined us wearing sweats and slippers, but with her eyes still painted. Josh made room on the sofa, but she squeezed onto the armchair with Tyler. That, I knew, was the start of trouble. From where I sat, I felt Josh's dead stare float past me on its way to the girl he'd paid, who had his money but who was clear across the room. I wondered, with some detachment, just how this'd go. But it didn't go anywhere yet. Instead, Josh tried to win the room with his magnetism. Noticing the girl beside him, he poked her hard in the ribs. He poked her again, jamming his finger into her tummy. She rubbed her side, confused.

"Say," he said. "Who's heard the one about the Chinaman well digger?"

I had, and knew Tyler had. Shoot, Josh told the joke every few weeks. But the girls waited for him to say it. Hitching straighter on the sofa, inviting attention, he said, "Well, so this farmer's dog, he falls in a well. Stands to reason chink well digger's responsible. So old boy, this farmer, drags his chink up the hill. 'You got to fetch my dog!' he yells. 'My dog's in the well!' Chink well digger, he peeks down in the darkness there, shaking his head. He says to the farmer, 'I no know. It hard job.' 'Hard job?' farmer says. 'What's so hard about fetching up a dog? Get down in that dark-ass well, and fetch my dog back!' 'No,' old chink says. 'Job very complex. Require much ketchup.'"

No one, Tyler and me excepted, realized the joke was finished. But Josh'd stopped talking, so the girls laughed from politeness. Josh himself, he howled like a hyena, looking everyone in the face, smacking his knee. "That's about as funny a joke as you'll hear," he said.

"It was funny," the girl beside him said.

"Them chinks'll eat dogs, raccoons, lizards, you name it."

One of the girls fetched beers from the kitchen. We drank those, sharing what was in the pipe. I didn't know what it was till years later. All I knew that night was it was electric. The smoke peeled my eyelids back over my head, till I wore them like a swim cap.

Kris wrapped her leg onto Tyler, purring and nuzzling like a kitty, and Josh, he tried hard with the other one, arm around her, whispering cowboy jokes. All the words in the room scratched at the inside of my skull, like claws. The colors, too. Kris rolled off Tyler, dragging him to his feet. They went upstairs, Tyler seeming bored with the fiasco but climbing those stairs behind her, sure enough. Josh pretended not to notice. He nibbled his girl's ear till she squirmed away, then wriggled along after her. I heard him whisper, "I think I'm falling for you," to go with other bullshit he likely whispered. But it was about then the girl beside me, who I'd realized was an Indian, pulled me off the sofa, leading me to another room.

The ways I'd imagined fucking all were versions of closeness, like passing through door after door you'd thought would be shut to you forever, till you couldn't believe how near the center you'd come, how nearly you were like everyone else. But fucking, it turned out, pushed *away* from the center, till you were farther off than ever.

I stood by the bed, watching this Indian girl push off her socks. She pushed down her drawers, lifted away her shirt, just mechanically like that. I undressed with her, thinking it wasn't so different than before football practice, taking off my school clothes. Naked, the girl climbed onto the mattress, on all fours. Even in the dark, I saw she wasn't what naked girls should look like. I'd seen magazines and videos, and knew girls in real life didn't resemble those they arranged for cameras. But I'd counted on shared characteristics at least, what with all girls belong to one biological species. It weren't so. The girl before me had bulges of herself where there oughtn't have been bulges, and her tits fully escaped her control. They weren't tits, so much as two tennis balls stuffed down in a pair of socks. I wondered—I wonder still—what this girl possibly thought of me. I couldn't have been what she wanted, my word.

"What's your favorite way?" she said, just directly like that. I didn't answer. Walking over on her knees, reaching for me, things got antsy and I flinched. She waited, and I put myself in her hand. Her touch wasn't gentle, and didn't carry messages like I'd hoped touching like that would've. Instead, it was like her digging in a drawer for something. Not finding it, she hauled her mouth onto me. I didn't like that. The girl was this big shadow in the room, and from that shadow I wicked just a dribble of wetness.

When I was how she wanted me, or as close to that as I'd get, the girl pulled me onto the bed to kiss my mouth. Her lips, I remember, were slick, and tasted like the smoke from earlier. She swung her leg past me, bending forward to turn her ass up in the dark. I didn't realize she'd reached under herself till something gripped me down there, making me flinch again. She put me right against her. "Go."

"Go?"

"Fuck me already. Hurry up."

I pushed some, then pushed farther and it was like the moment pushing a truck from mud, when nothing happens then it gives. "Oh," the girl said, me slipping fully into her. With nowhere to place them, I set my hands on her ass. The girl was bigger in my hands than I'd reckoned with my eyes. And it was happening then, back and forth, and even happening in a manner I'd imagined, from behind like that, her kneeling forward. And it felt good to be fucking, absolutely it did. As a physical sensation, nothing beat it.

But it wasn't long till the moment fell apart. I thought initially it was the odor. No one'd told me fucking had an odor, and certainly magazines and videos weren't helpful in that regard. But pussy had a stench to it. It came in waves, these tangy, sharp pangs that brought to mind rusty drinking fountains. It wasn't the odor, though, really. Really, the problem was me, who I was. Fucking, I'd believed, would mean I was all right. I was good enough someone'd fuck me, leastways. But, kneeling there, it was the same Michael James with his same folds and pudge, his same arms and hands with no interest to them—arms and hands of blank fat. I wasn't all right. I was me. Truthfully, I was even more me, more emphasized, on account of the fucking. Like fucking was what I might've been, if I were something better, while here instead was actual me, Michael James in the flesh, some tubby hick wailing away at a stranger.

Anyhow, I couldn't connect my fucking and my dreams, which it turns out you have to do. I went soft, a problem I'd heard about but had thought would be the least of my worries. We wound down, this Indian and I, like a thing low on batteries, and laid there. After a time, she fetched me a pill from her drawer. She said I needed it with what we'd smoked earlier. "Fine," I said. She said she didn't care about the fucking. "It's just a fuck," was how she put it. I didn't care about it any more than she did, I just wished I felt better.

The smoke, the pill, the liquor—I lay in the darkness in a suspended nausea, weaving in and out of sleep. When the shouting started, I thought at first I was dreaming it. Then I thought it was the Russian from earlier, that we'd overshot our time. But I'd slept only a few minutes. We had more time, and by God we'd need it. The shouting was Josh. I pulled on my jeans, stumbling to the door, the Indian girl mumbling, trying to collect herself.

In the living room, Josh knelt on the sofa, the girl pinned underneath him. He reared back like he was starting a lawnmower, then crashed his fist into her; the sound was like dropping a steak on the floor. She'd been shrieking, but the hit stopped her flat.

"That better?" Josh screamed. He reared again, but I held his arms, pulling him off her. "Fucking liar!" he screamed. The girl slumped to the floor just as the Indian girl, still naked, ran in to help. She knelt with her friend, touching the blood. "Emma?" she said. "Emma?"

Kris appeared in bra and sweats, and threw herself on the floor. "Em?" Her hands fluttered at the hurt girl's face, like birds figuring where to land. Tyler came downstairs, shirt unbuttoned. I had Josh by the arms, but he shrugged me off and paced the wall, glaring at the girls.

"The fuck happened?" Tyler said.

"He's fucking crazy," said the Indian. Tyler told her to shut up.

"She wouldn't do it," Josh said.

Tyler looked at him. "Wouldn't do what?"

"Oh, come on, Tyler, Jesus. You know it's what's fair."

Tyler rubbed his forehead. "Christ, Joshy."

"I'm not paying and not getting it."

"She's not a *whore*!" screamed the Indian. Josh lunged at her, but Tyler stepped between them, walking him back. Josh pointed over Tyler's shoulder. "I want my fucking money!"

"No," Tyler said. "That's their money. They're keeping it."

Kris held the hurt girl's face, but beyond holding it seemed unsure what to do. She glanced at her hands, the blood on them. "Fuck it," she said. "Fuck this." She knelt at her purse, digging through it.

"Call him," the Indian said. "Call Viktor."

"Fuck Viktor, I'm calling the cops."

She dialed, but Tyler left Josh where he stood and took the phone from her hand, closed it. He seemed sad, I remember, like all at once he realized what we'd have to do. Kris reached for the phone. When she reached again, Tyler slapped her hard. "Sit on the fucking couch," he said. "You too." Kris and the Indian glanced at each other, then did as told. For the first time, I had a view of the girl Josh hit. I remember thinking: That face isn't the shape it was before. He bent that face.

Tyler stared at the girl. "Fuck, get her up there with you. Try to..." He shook his head.

The three of us watching, Kris and the Indian lifted their friend by her armpits, her head swinging and blood roping from her eye. They held her upright on the sofa, or mostly upright. She moaned, and I realized then it was truly possible the girl'd die. Lord, and she may've died. I can't say positively she didn't.

With a *crack*, Tyler snapped Kris's phone in his hands, tossed aside the pieces. Nodding at the hurt girl, he said, "She got one?" Kris dug the phone from her friend's pocket, and surrendered it to Tyler. He broke that like he'd broken the first, and stood there thinking. I thought, too. I thought I should go in the bedroom to break the Indian's phone, which'd be in her sweats. I thought Kris and the Indian, if we didn't gag them, would scream, and that neighbors'd come, or call police. I wondered what we could find to use on them. But then I remembered there'd been screaming already, and that screaming in that part of town wouldn't be unusual. No—no one was coming through that door to help anybody.

Tyler crouched, arms hanging off his knees, staring at the floor. Behind him, Josh fidgeted and paced, hands worrying his pockets. "Man, we need something," he said. "We *need* something."

"Just leave," Kris said. "It's not like we know you."

Tyler shook his head.

"We won't talk," the Indian said. She looked awful like that, naked and scared and that drinking fountain odor still in my mind. She said again they wouldn't talk. Tyler told her to shut up. "I'm thinking," he said.

All of us were quiet, the three of them on the sofa, and Josh and me standing behind Tyler. The girl revived some, watching us with her spared eye. But there wasn't sight in that eye, not really. The world poured through it and out the other side. What needed to happen formed in my mind then. I wished my mind weren't where it formed, but certain people, given any circumstance, discover automatically their own advantage, like water in a cracked glass finds its crack, and seeps out. I wished I weren't such a person, but it came with being smart, and with being a coward.

I didn't say it right off. I hoped Tyler'd say it first, to save my conscience. But I was worried what Josh'd do if we lingered there. So I said, "One of them's got a kid, Ty. There's a kid here."

He looked at me.

"There's toys all around. Someone's got a kid."

"You son of a bitch," the Indian said.

I couldn't look at her. I said to Tyler, "Just have her show it to us. That's enough."

Studying the Indian, Tyler seemed to get it. I glanced at Josh. He didn't get it, but his part in this was over.

The girl cried in her hands, naked and shaking. I thought, as Tyler dragged her off, demanding she show him the kid: You know what, this is best for everyone. Everyone wins with this. These people should thank me.

The kid was up the street. Tyler described it later. Little thing slept in its crib, nursery music playing, and because Tyler couldn't think what else to do, he showed the Indian the .44 from his dad's truck. He said that's what he'd use if she talked, if any of them did. Walking back inside, he held the pistol in the crib, showing what he meant. She cried and cried, which Tyler took as a positive sign. Back at the duplex, waiting, we sat without watching each other. The doorbell rang. Josh jumped to his feet, fidgeting, gripping and releasing his jeans. Kris said relax. "It's just Connor," she said.

We'd turned off the lights. A shadow appeared on the curtain, this Connor peering in.

"The fuck's he doing?" Josh whispered.

"Nothing. He wants to smoke."

"He'd better not come in here."

"He'll go away," she said. "Relax."

He did. The next shadow on the window was Tyler, leading the Indian by her arm. Inside, he threw her on the sofa. We wanted to tape the girls' wrists, but couldn't find tape, so we just reminded them what we were willing to do.

Tyler nodded at the hurt girl, slumped there with her friends. "Little black eye be the least of your worries," he said.

Some days later, we wrecked the truck. Probably we didn't need to, but the girls'd seen it, as had the Russian and whoever else, and it was the truck Mr. Copeland drove to town twice a week. Spokane wasn't so big you could bet against a coincidence. Anyways, the insurance money'd cover it. We took it into the pine woods south of Cheney. Tyler and I watching, Josh climbed behind the wheel, buckled his belt and raced the engine. He saluted out the window, which Tyler and I ignored. "Go on and do it!" Tyler shouted. Kneading the wheel, nodding, Josh floored it. The tires spun, smoking. Bed skating sideways, the truck squatted and took off. Josh got himself to speed—30 or 40 miles an-hour—then lined the right headlamp into a Ponderosa near the shoulder. The impact tore that side of the truck, spinning Josh so he faced the tree, like a wheeling dog. Steam hissed, shit leaking everyplace, but he trotted away healthy as a doe. As he was fond of saying, he lived under a lucky star.

But that first morning, getting back to Edwall, we didn't know what to do about the truck or about anything. It was dawn. No one wanted to go home, so we sat in the diner on Main Street. But no one wanted to talk, either, so we sat with our pancakes, no one eating, no one looking anywhere but out the windows. It was the same diner it'd always been, on the same Main Street, the same folks outside strolling in sunlight. I'd known those people all my life. But they were changed somehow. Their faces were. I get now, of course, that I was changed, and they only appeared different because I saw them from a new vantage. But all I got then—and that just dimly—was someday, on a dark day, the wrong door'd open, and there wasn't much that'd keep me from stepping through it.

Annika and the Hulk

Her arrest was noted in the Legals section of *The Spokesman Review*, which I wouldn't have been reading except I had a treatment that morning. On treatment days, I read the newspaper thoroughly, each word of it like a step into the tunnel I'm fleeing down, until Ted, the nurse, catches my elbow and walks me back to the La-Z-Boy recliners and IV caddies, where, as Ted puts it, "The magic happens." Annika Byers, age twenty-four. She'd been arrested for "gross misdemeanor theft"—a challenging phrase to deduce severity from. On the one hand, she'd merely committed a misdemeanor. On the other, it was gross. I rotated the newspaper in my hands, as if that'd improve my perspective on the matter. Then I folded the paper on the table and placed my spectacles on top of it and watched them.

I knew she wasn't my niece. The last name was wrong, for one thing. But then again, maybe she was my niece. How many Annikas lived in Spokane, after all, and how many were the age of my brother's daughter? I read the notice again, and then folded the paper in my lap and watched the other patients shuffle among the sofas and televisions of the leisure area. I read the notice a third time. Really the last name didn't mean anything. She might've married or changed her name, and frankly I wasn't sure what last name she'd been given to begin with. Certainly Robert, my brother, had never married the girl's mother. None of us had met that woman. Perhaps she was a Byers?

We also had never met Annika, not even when she was little, and truthfully it was possible she didn't exist. There'd just been a rumor after my brother's death that he'd fathered a daughter and her name was Annika. I'd looked into it and never found anything. But Robert had lived throughout the area and mostly in destitute circles. It was possible a child of his would've escaped the system's notice, and perhaps even his own.

The clock in the leisure area is a cat—they try to keep us cheerful—and according to the cat's paws, I had forty-five minutes before my treatment. Missing it would mean Tammy, my wife, would crucify me, and really I had no reason to miss it—Robert had been dead twenty years and whatever I'd felt about my brother was settled now. But Annika, and her being in trouble—reading that was like a door opening where before there'd been a wall. I can't explain it any better than that. It just felt important that I walk through the door. And anyway, Tammy was home in Helena and couldn't stop me, and also this was my fourth battery of treatments in two years—crucifixion wasn't seeming like such an unappealing alternative.

I found Ted in the hall. "I'm going to take a bath," I said.

"You got it, Hulk," he said. He's assigned each of us the name of a superhero.

I walked downstairs and out of the building.

The Spokane County Jail is a tall structure with slits for windows, making it look like a huge surge protector, and apart from the Cancer Center it was the one building in town I was familiar with. Clerks at the jail had often called me when Robert was arrested—he wouldn't call, but the clerks would—and I would drive over from Montana to see about my brother. Always it was some trifling offense for which Robert's bail was \$500 or \$1,000, and always I would pay the sum without troubling with a bondsman, both because it was faster and because if Robert skipped bail I didn't want a bondsman tracking me down. Bells would ring in the corridors and gates would slide open and slam, and there my brother would be in the rags they'd arrested him in, shambling along beside a bailiff. He knew the clerks and bailiffs and conversed with them pleasantly, though to me, he wouldn't say a word. I'd follow him outside and he'd disappear somewhere in the dark. I guess he made his court dates? They kept allowing him bail, at any rate, though no penny of that money ever came back to me.

That'd been a lifetime ago, but it was eerie climbing the jailhouse steps that morning in the rain. The steps weren't so steep, but I rested partway up and then again at the top, just taking a moment with the handrail. The humiliation of treatment, let me tell you, isn't losing your hair or walking around like a Halloween skeleton—it's not even knowing that when you die everyone will see you in your casket that way, though I admit that's not a joyful proposition. It's the helplessness. It's needing Ted's assistance when I climb off the toilet and it's resting twice on a flight of eight steps. A man in a suit, I suppose an attorney, trotted up the steps behind me and I pretended my furlough at the handrail was to admire my view of Spokane, dreary as it was.

The clerk that day was a black woman with tattoos on her knuckles whose face I didn't recognize. Of course I wouldn't have recognized her—she'd have been no more than a toddler when last I'd visited the jail. Just the same, I was disappointed. Somehow, I'd expected a familiar face behind the desk, someone who'd remember me and what I'd gone through with my brother, and who'd understand effortlessly the connection between those visits and what I was there for today. Not that I fully understood that connection. Not that someone who did recall me from 1989 would stand a chance at recognizing me now. Some weeks earlier in Helena, I'd passed on the street a man I'd worked with for six years, and he'd looked directly at me and kept walking.

I told the woman at the desk I wished to see Annika Byers. She smacked her gum at me. "All right," she said and did nothing.

"Can I see her?" I said.

"Who?"

I repeated the name. The woman appeared not to have heard me, but finally she drew a tolerant breath and tapped keys on her keyboard. She put a phone to her ear and smacked her gum and waited.

I'd never visited anyone in jail. With Robert, I'd merely written checks and watched him disappear into the night. After he died, I realized I ought to have visited him. My checks, obviously, hadn't amounted to much by way of getting him on his feet, even as they'd amounted to a great deal where dollar figures were concerned. Perhaps visiting him would've produced some results? Probably, if I'm being honest with myself, Robert wouldn't have consented to see me—prisoners, like millionaires, can dispatch guards like butlers to dismiss unwelcome callers—but I ought to have tried, and with his daughter I was going to try. Or with his maybe daughter. His plausibly daughter. I imagined a pane of glass would separate us, and that we'd speak through a pair of black telephones on the wall, but the bailiff showed me into a room with folding chairs and fluorescent lights. He sat me there while he fetched Annika.

Bells rang somewhere in the building, a sound I remembered, and into the room walked a woman I perceived at once bore no resemblance to my brother—where his hair had been black, hers was red; where his eyes brown, hers green. Finally, her face was gaunt and angular. No one in our family had a face like that (until me, recently). But toward this woman I felt immediately a warm flood of kinship.

"Annika," I said, and when I stood to embrace her the bailiff laid a hand on my shoulder and returned me to my chair. The woman wouldn't have welcomed the embrace, anyway—she peered at me like I was a lunatic. But she'd never met me, so some skepticism was warranted. She sat uneasily.

"I'm Edward," I explained. I glanced at the bailiff to see if handshakes were permissible, and he shook his head. With no other tools at my disposal, I sat forward on the chair and tried to project congeniality, grinning and rubbing my palms. "I'm your uncle," I said.

It was like she'd never heard that word. "What?"

"You are Annika, correct? Byers?"

She nodded slowly.

"I don't know how to tell you this." I laughed. "Except I guess I already told you. I'm your uncle. I'm Robert's brother."

Since resuming treatment, I've grown sensitive to odors. Particularly, I notice foods I loved once that now nauseate me, like garlic, but at that moment I detected on Annika the cheap soap she used, and her sour breath. Rather than nausea, however, her scent inspired in me a kind of guardianship not unlike what parents must feel over helpless infants, the sense that if they don't protect this creature no one will.

"Who's Robert?" Annika asked.

"You knew him as Bob, I guess. Or I guess you knew him as Dad." Again I laughed at myself. Meeting Annika was cheerful, somehow, even if this was a jail and she a thief and I deep into chemo. Even if our sole affiliation was a transient who'd discharged a pistol into his forehead rather than face trial for breaking and entering.

Annika laughed with me. "I don't know any Bobs, man. No Roberts either. Except maybe on TV."

"We're talking about your dad," I said.

She shook her head. "Well, I don't know him, either."

I sat back in my chair. It made sense that she wouldn't know Robert, sad as that was.

"Look." The woman shifted on her chair, causing the bailiff to step forward. She lifted her wrists, which were cuffed. "I don't know who the fuck you are, okay? But I'm not your little girl or whatever."

"I think you are, Annika. You're my niece."

"My dad's name's Tyler," she said. "He's a junkie in Portland."

"He was a junkie. He's actually dead now."

Annika was silent. Hearing your father's dead is hard no matter who he was or what your relationship with him had been. It's hard even if there'd been no relationship—perhaps especially hard. I gave her a minute. The expression on her face wasn't what I'd have expected—it was more contemplative than grief-stricken, as if she were pondering an enigma. But there's no accounting for how we process loss.

"I'm sorry," I said.

"So you're here," Annika said, "because you're sad about your brother."

"Well, not that exactly. He's been dead for years. I'm here about you."

"About me."

"I want to help, Annika."

We were silent a moment, the fluorescent lights humming above us and the concrete corridors muffling within them some faint shouting.

"And how do you want to help," Annika said.

"For one thing, I want to get you out of here. We'll start with that. And I don't know your circumstances, but I could help with those."

"So money," she said.

"That'd be part of it."

She watched me awhile, then seemed to decide something. She studied her fingernails and smiled.

"It wouldn't be free," I said.

"Of course not."

"There'd be conditions. You need to improve things, Annika. You need to straighten yourself out."

"But you'd help me," she said.

I nodded. "Yes."

She laughed a little, lifting her wrists to scratch her earlobe. She dropped her hands in her lap. "Well," she said. "Let's get out of this dump."

"So you accept?"

"Accept what?"

"The conditions," I said.

"Oh," she said. "Yeah."

The bailiff led Annika away, then returned and showed me into an office to process payment. The bail was $11,000—Annika had prior convictions. Watching me write the check, the bailiff said, "Sir, are you absolutely positive..."

"What?" I said.

The man reconsidered. "Forget it."

***

The first thing Annika wanted was the farthest thing from my mind, and that was food, but we drove to a diner near the jail, in the part of Spokane where Annika said she'd grown up and lived now. It was a grim, depleted district with plywood nailed over windows and yards stuffed with weeds. In some of the yards, muscle-bound dogs paced on chains. Where homes had burned—I saw at least three such homes—the surviving walls were streaked with soot, as if the rain were washing away mascara. And here and there walked derelict individuals oblivious to the rain, some of whom were old enough to have known my brother, perhaps, when he was such an individual walking such streets. Not that any of those souls, living how they lived, would've remembered an acquaintance from that long ago.

Annika wore the ragged jeans and hooded sweatshirt she'd been arrested in. As we coasted along, her gaze drifted onto me and away again, and then returned and again drifted away. I couldn't fault her curiosity. A relative materializing in your life jars you, and casts your known relatives in new light and shadow. I knew that because I was undergoing the same experience.

Annika's gaze landed on me and stayed. "That was a lot of money."

"Well," I said, "I'll get it back."

"That must be something, throwing around that kind of money."

I laughed. "I agree. I wonder what it feels like for someone who can afford to do it."

"What?"

"I mean that's money I need back, Annika. I'm not 'throwing it around.'"

She thought about that. "Well, but you have it. You put it up for me."

"I suppose that's true."

My niece watched me, then gazed at passing houses. "You wouldn't have put it up if you didn't have it."

We arrived at a blue building with glass block windows, a Pepsi sign with faded lettering hanging crooked over the door. To the left of that door was a door papered with condemnation notices. Eating in a condemned building wasn't an appetizing thought, but then again, for me, nothing was appetizing. Annika led us into a dining room of Formica and vinyl and linoleum, with wrestling trophies cluttering the walls. There were stools occupied by men who glanced at us, then sipped their coffee and forgot us. I'd thought Annika would know people there, but that wasn't the case. We took a booth at the back of the room, where other booths had been ripped out, exposing rectangles of particle board subflooring.

"I could eat a racehorse," Annika announced, sliding into the booth and plucking a menu from behind the napkin holder. The air in the diner was humid with grease, and it took everything I had not to wretch. But I was glad she was hungry. In the diner's bad lighting, her skin was sallow and her eyes dark and baggy—eating would do her good. A cook in a stained apron brought plastic cups of water, and I wondered what I looked like in that dismal lighting. Maybe like one of those Mexican skeletons wandering around like he isn't already dead.

The cook brought biscuits, which Annika slathered with butter and began tucking away like she was racing a clock. "God," she said, resting and chewing. "The thing with jail. You get so hungry, and they just have that road kill to eat in there."

"Well," I said, "eat up. Eating's important."

She worked butter onto another biscuit.

"Though we should probably—"

"Where is that guy?" Annika craned her neck to see into the kitchen and waved her arm over her head until the cook returned. She ordered bacon and waffles and French toast and coffee. I told the man I'd already eaten. Annika added sausage to her order, along with orange juice and an egg.

When the cook left, I said, "We should talk about a plan, Annika. So we can decide what you need."

She nodded. "I know. And believe me, I want a plan. I just think I need to eat first, you know? If I have some energy, we can make a good plan."

I watched her polish off the biscuits, and then lick a finger and course it around the plate for crumbs. She looked up at me. "Oh God!" She laughed. "Did you want one?"

"No," I said.

"We'll get more."

"What's your living situation, Annika? Can you tell me that?"

She climbed from the booth and carried the plate around the counter into the kitchen. She was gone awhile, during which time I heard her visiting with the cook but missed what exactly they said. At one point Annika did say, "Man, you've got to have something! What're you holding?" and laughed so loudly that it rang off the equipment back there. But I didn't hear what else passed between them. Annika returned carrying biscuits and two mugs of coffee.

"He's almost finished," she said. "It looks delicious back there. And look, I got you coffee!"

"Annika," I said. "Can you tell me about where you live? Is it safe?"

"What's that?"

"We need to figure this stuff out."

Annika laughed. "Ed," she said. "And I guess it's Uncle Ed, huh? Can't this wait, Uncle Ed? We don't even know each other! Come on, relax. Tell me about Dad."

"I'm trying to help."

"Uncle Ed." Annika laid a palm on her chest. "I know that. And I know I've made mistakes in life and I know I'm lucky you're here. But stuff like this takes time, you know? So let's take our time. I want to hear about my dad! I bet he was great, huh?"

She stirred sugar and cream into her coffee, and when she looked up a vestige of Robert passed over her features. I'd been looking for a likeness between them and this was it. Annika wore on her face that same expression Robert had worn late in life, once he'd decided things were a certain way and he'd no longer entertain alternate interpretations. As expressions went, it was as amiable as it was impenetrable; it was the smirk that'd dead-ended every conversation I'd had with my brother in his final years.

Suddenly, I could've strangled Annika, but the cook appeared with plates balanced up his arms and began unloading them before her, and so awful was the stench of the food that I couldn't focus on strangulation or on anything else. The waffles smelled like the boxes they'd shipped in, and the maple syrup Annika drizzled over everything released an essence of meat drippings, as if the syrup had been used to clean a skillet. My mouth seeped bile. I pressed a napkin to my lips, closed my eyes and tried to breathe.

"What's a good Dad story?" Annika said. I parted my eyes and watched her saw at her French toast. She hunted for butter packets, and finally grabbed some from a neighboring table. "I want to hear all about him. You probably loved him, huh? He was your brother."

I removed the napkin from my mouth but replaced it immediately, like a valve cap. The bile swelled and I stumbled from the booth, making my way through the dining room to the door. Outside, the rain had stopped and I sucked hard at the damp air to wash back the nausea. It was a strategy that worked sometimes, but between inhalations the queasiness worsened, and I circled into the alley and was sick against the side of the building. I wretched again, the vomit a yellow froth, and for a time I leaned there letting moments pass. What returned me to myself was my phone ringing. I didn't want to answer, but if I ignored Tammy, she'd call the police and the fire department and the FBI and Catholic Church.

I put the phone to my ear. "Hi, sweetheart."

"Edward Leroy. Where in God's name are you?"

"Calm down."

"I won't calm down. The clinic says you disappeared?"

"I said calm down."

"Where are you?" she said.

"I'm here. I had to see about something."

"Here?"

"I'm in Spokane."

"What did you have to see about that trumps chemo, Edward?"

"Forget it, okay? You found me. I'm fine."

The line was silent.

"I'm fine," I said again.

There was a racket in the street and a beeping sound; a garbage truck rumbled into the alley. "Edward?" Tammy said. "Edward, what is that?"

I walked ahead of the truck and turned down another alley. "What's that sound?" Tammy demanded to know.

"Listen." I rubbed my forehead and breathed and tried to relax. "There's something I had to do, all right? I'm not explaining it now."

"What'd you have to do?"

"Jesus," I said.

"You can't expect me to giggle and hang up, Edward."

"That is what I expect, Tamara. That is what I expect. And I'm not spending another minute dealing with this. If they call, cancel my appointments."

"Cancel them?"

A door on the back of the building opened, and Annika emerged into the alley. Not noticing me, she started toward the street.

"Edward?" my wife said. "Edward? Listen, I'm coming out there. You need to—"

I closed the phone and dropped it into my pocket. "Where're you going?" I shouted.

Annika jolted and doubled over, patting her chest. I walked toward her. "Were you leaving?" I said.

"You scared the shit out of me."

"We had a deal."

"No," she said. "I just—I didn't have money. You left. I didn't know what to do."

My phone was ringing.

"I thought he'd call the police. The diner guy."

She was lying and my phone was ringing and the nausea was swelling again; I shouldn't have wasted myself shouting in the alley and getting impatient with my wife. I was lightheaded. My phone was ringing.

"Should you get that?" Annika said.

"Be quiet."

She held out her hand. "Give me some money. I'll pay, you can see who it is."

I silenced the phone and led Annika back into the diner. While we waited at the register, she drummed her hands on the counter and rocked onto the balls of her feet and off again. "So what now?" she said. "I think we need clothes and stuff. Like for interviews. Also, I need lady stuff."

"You're going to show me where you live," I said.

Annika's house was a dilapidated Victorian some decades past habitability, with wilting dormers and tattered siding and a dirt yard littered with rusted debris and trash and birdfeeders, and before even arriving there I was exhausted from an incident that'd transpired at the convenience store around the corner, where we'd stopped so my niece could buy tampons. It was the kind of decrepit store with mounds in the parking area where gas pumps had been torn out, and a storm fence cluttered with beer and cigarette ads. There was a phone booth near the fence with the phone and phone directory missing. Against my better judgment, I'd given Annika ten dollars. It was hardly enough to misbehave with, and if she said she needed lady stuff I guess I had to trust her. But after some time she hadn't come out of the store and I knew she'd gone ahead and misbehaved all that she could on that ten bucks.

I went inside and glanced around and finally approached the Sikh dozing at the register. "Did you see a woman come in here? Red hair?" I said. The store was a cramped labyrinth of wheeled shelves and clutter, and Annika could've been anywhere. The man blinked drowsily and glanced down the counter at a corridor leading to the back. "Back there?" I said. I followed the corridor and found a locked restroom with light glowing under the door. "Annika?" I knuckled the door. "Annika?" I said again.

"Occupied!" she shouted.

"What're you doing in there?"

"Uncle Edward! You didn't say you were that kind of uncle."

Something glass rattled in the bathroom, and Annika muttered to herself. I knocked again, and when she didn't answer I returned to the register. "Where's the key?" I asked the Sikh.

He gestured down the corridor. "She has it."

"Where's yours?"

"That is mine," he said.

Back at the restroom, I tried the knob and shouldered the door. Pain bloomed through me, and the door didn't give. "Would you come out, please?"

"I'm using the toilet! Be done in a minute!"

Exhausted, I sat on a milk crate in the corridor and waited. I wanted to tell Annika I was calling the police, and see what she did about that. But using the restroom isn't a crime even if you're out on bail, and even if it were I wouldn't have called the police and Annika knew it. I waited. The Sikh dozed again. Eventually the toilet flushed, which would've been a clever touch had Annika been a teenager smoking cigarettes in the bathroom, instead of a grown woman throwing her life away. The door opened and she tottered past me in an atmosphere of alcohol. On the bathroom floor stood a drained bottle of fortified wine and, to my niece's credit, what appeared to be a tampon wrapper. What could I do? I walked Annika, swaying slightly, to my car and drove her home.

The house was disgraceful from the curb and inside was worse. No light switches were operable and grimy curtains fluttered at shattered windows. Boot and animal tracks covered the floor, and despite the breeze from the smashed windows there hung in the house a rank musk of urine and other waste. The place appeared deserted. Annika staggered past me and fell onto a sofa with exposed stuffing, her shoes soiling the cushions. "We're taking a little snooze," she said.

I could've used a snooze, but instead grasped Annika by her wrists and pulled her upright.

"No," she said.

"We're fixing this."

"What?"

"We're cleaning this place. This is your house, Annika."

"Jesus," she said. "Give it a break."

"You can't live like this."

She tore her wrists free and lay back on the sofa with an arm covering her eyes. "You're not Mother Theresa, all right? People have shitty houses. Deal with it."

"Not you," I said.

"No, me, actually. I'm one of the shitty-house people."

Annika dug her shoulders into the cushions, then rolled onto her side. A curtain billowed over the sofa and settled, and outside I heard rain pattering. The room was dark with dark wallpaper, except where older wallpaper showed through like fish scales. The floors were filmy, and wrappers and scraps of paper fluttered around. The house couldn't be cleaned—not by me nor Annika nor anyone. The place was entirely lost. Still, something had to be done about it. I began feeling in my blood and lungs an electricity the doctors had warned me about, an electricity they said was false, that I oughtn't trust. "It's your Hulk strength," Ted had said. "And it's about as real as the green guy himself. You feel that, just sit down. It'll take you about five feet and drop you."

But something had to be done about Annika's house, and I felt strong. Hunting through the rooms, I found rags and some jugs of bleach (which I doubted had been used for laundry). I piled the rags in the bathtub and poured bleach over them. I went back to Annika.

"Get up," I said.

When Annika didn't stir, I hauled her off of the sofa by her ankles. She muttered and cursed, and as she slid to the floor she kicked at me halfheartedly.

"You're going to take care of your house," I said.

"It's fine."

"Here." I gathered from the coffee table an armful of Styrofoam cups and paper plates and empty cigarette packages. I heaped it all on the floor where Annika was sitting, and then gathered more trash from a recliner across the room and added that to the pile. "Take this outside. Take it somewhere. Get rid of it."

"Man, that's Seth. He's a slob," Annika said.

"I don't care whose it is. Get rid of it."

Annika's chin dropped to her chest. Finally, she rolled onto her knees and started picking at the waste. "Good," I told her. "Good!" On the hearth was some clutter that perhaps wasn't trash—mismatched silverware and CD cases and earphones and knit gloves—but to preserve momentum, I swept all of it into a Taco Bell sack, along with some napkins and plastic liquor bottles and lighters and junk mail envelopes. I harried Annika to her feet with the waste she was holding and led her outside to the trashcans in the alley. "Bit by bit," I said as we walked back. "Bit by bit, and you'll have a place worth living in. That's where your life starts."

"Ed," she said.

"Shut up. I don't want to hear it."

Some dozen loads later, we'd cleared the living room of trash, if you didn't count the trash that passed as furniture. The rain hadn't let up and both of us were soaked through our clothes and shivering. We'd tracked fresh mud into the house. A headache had seeped down my neck toward the aches and nausea rising to meet it. But the living room was clear. We'd accomplished that much. Next, I decided, we'd scrub the living room floor. We'd clean just the one room to completion so it stood as an example. "Okay," I said. "Let's get our shoes off and get them in the hall."

Annika slumped. "Ed, I'm not doing this anymore."

"Take your shoes off. Take them out in the hall."

"No," she said. "No, this is stupid. You're not going to make me a Christian or whatever. You're wasting your time."

"Take your shoes off."

"Look, I'm saving you the trouble. I said that shit about conditions? Ed, that was a lie. That was bullshit."

I heeled off my own shoes and carried them into the hall, then returned and started pushing sofas against the walls.

"Are you listening?" Annika said. "Are you hearing this? Look, I'm sorry about your brother but I'm not—look, I wanted out of fucking jail, man."

But even as Annika spoke, she slipped off her shoes and tossed them into the hall.

"Get this furniture out of the way," I said, then went in the bathroom where the rags were soaking. I doused them a second time, then carried them back into the living room with bleach dripping on my socks. I dumped the rags in a heap on the floor.

"Take a few of these and get started," I said. "It's going to hurt the wood but we're not worried about the wood."

I took a rag to the foyer and knelt and began scrubbing at the animal tracks. They wouldn't lift, so I retrieved the bleach and poured it onto the floor directly, a spectral stain spreading as the fluid ran out over the floorboards. Annika selected one of the rags and stood with it dangling from her fingers.

"Let's go," I remember saying, though I was kneeling over the bleach and scrubbing and the fumes of the bleach had moved into my nostrils and mind. The daylight in the windows sucked away.

When I awoke, the chill from being wet and the hollowness of not eating, along with my general exhaustion, crashed into me like vehicles sailing into a pileup, and in the darkness I could scarcely move. A faint band of light split crosswise through my vision. I thought something in my eyes had gone haywire, but then I saw it was light falling in through an open door. As I watched, the light dampened and guttered, and from the direction of the light there floated a chorus of muttering voices.

I managed to sit upright, and waited on the bed while my strength recovered. Across from me, on the floor, I perceived my shoes and wallet and phone, the screen of which lit up and dimmed again. The bed was misshapen and heaped with oily blankets. Soiled shirts strung on twine covered the windows. My phone illuminated again, and hobbling over to it, I discovered the disturbances were voicemails and messages from my wife, whole confetti loads of them saying everything you'd imagine. My wallet, predictably, was devoid of cash and credit cards. I stepped into my shoes and loaded my effects into my pockets. I moved up the hall toward the voices and candlelight.

Seven or eight of them were sprawled in the room I'd attempted to clean, though now that cleaning seemed only a feverish nightmare. The people were corpselike, and worse, and were passing between them several ugly needles on a tray. Observing me in the doorway, a vacant-eyed boy with caved cheeks said, "Fuck, he's alive."

The group stirred toward awareness but subsided far short of it. The boy who'd spoken kept his eyes fastened on me, though it was clear the vision behind his eyes had dissolved.

"Where's Annika?" I said.

One of them tilted his head back gradually, like the long draw of a pumpjack, and then remained like that with his eyes lidded and mouth gaping at the ceiling. No one else responded even to that degree. I walked out of the house.

There was no reason my car would be there, and it wasn't, and so I set out on foot toward the store we'd visited earlier. That seemed like a street where things happened. Maybe I'd find Annika there. It was a cold night, and shivering in my damp clothes, I saw that the clouds had blown off. Stars reeled overhead. Passing a dark house, I heard a chain pay out over the yard, but the dog stopped short of me and simply watched, its eyes slits of streetlight. I wouldn't eat me either, I supposed. A door banged somewhere and somewhere else glass shattered and a man laughed wildly.

Nothing was happening at the store. The Sikh's turbaned head floated alone in the window, surrounded by tobacco and lottery tickets. Novelty sweatshirts hung in the window, and I thought to buy one to get warm before remembering my money was gone. And I'd been wrong about the street. No one was about on foot, and in every direction from the intersection stretched long vectors of streetlights under which nothing stirred. I picked a direction and started out, thinking that Annika had to be somewhere. The more ground I covered, the higher was my likelihood of finding her.

I walked, and as I walked I imagined that each block was a length of rope I took up. At the other end of that rope, I decided, I'd find my brother's daughter. Maybe it was the chills, but I imagined that, when I found her, Annika would be holding in her arms the wrecked contraption that was her life. She'd spill that life into my arms like it was a sick child. I covered ten blocks, then twenty. Feeling that false electricity, a dull pulse of it, I started the count over and reached twenty a second time, passing into a neighborhood of nicer homes. The sky paled. The city kept unfolding, as if my walking the streets multiplied them. I produced my phone, but tapping the buttons forgot who I meant to call. Then somehow I misplaced my phone, or dropped it. The stars vanished, and soon traffic was sailing by, commuter traffic. I fell in someone's lawn.

There's exhaustion past which nothing exists, or might as well not. I wanted to do more, to find Annika and save her. I wanted my brother not to have been an obdurate man and me not to have been helpless with him. But those things were beyond me, those and many others. The trees overhead were a gray stillness spanned by the farthest blue. I heard a screen door slam and footsteps, and remembered a morning I'd spent with Robert decades ago—decades before he'd found trouble, before it even seemed like he'd find it. We were swimming at the beach in McCall, Idaho, where we'd grown up. It was one of those years in Idaho where summer ends in August and the mountains start accumulating snow. But we'd swum anyway, despite the cold, and now we ran onto the beach shivering and hugging ourselves. I'd brought towels. I wrapped in one and roughed myself, and as Robert ran up, I tossed him the other. There was no reason he should've refused it—it was the second towel and there were only two of us—but he tossed back what I'd offered and instead shivered and stamped his feet.

It wouldn't be the last time in my life that I reached for my brother and touched stone. But lying that morning, in that person's lawn, Robert wasn't stone, somehow. Not anymore. He wasn't proud. He was a boy who'd become a man and died, just as everyone did, and all I could give him then, and perhaps could ever have given him, was my feeling about him, and he'd had that and had it still. We'd swum together in a frigid lake, if nothing else. It's not that it was all right so much as that it had to be all right. It was all the two of us would get.

A stranger knelt over me, peering down from his concerned face. He touched my shoulder. A great deal, I realized, was as all right as it would ever be.

Common Tongue

Underclassmen weren't permitted to leave campus, but every day after fourth period Barry Laird left anyhow and walked the six blocks to Castle Rock Apartments, where he ate lunch and prayed with his mother and brother, Rhett. This was in Billings, where Deborah Laird had moved with her boys after Martin, their father, was killed in a highway accident. He'd been a steadfast provider, Martin had, and had purchased the family a home on twenty acres in Bridger, Montana, where they'd raised small livestock and crops and most importantly had educated their boys not at a public school, but on the screened porch adjoining their kitchen, with Deborah instructing. That'd been the preferable way for Rhett and Barry to learn, because at home they could pray during lessons (which Rimrock High, in Billings, didn't value), and because Deborah knew her sons intimately and could instruct them according to their anointed natures, without fashioning them into secularists. But Martin had believed, as his wife and sons also believed, the profit a man wrought from the earth—or, from his asphalt business in Laurel, with locations opening in Casper and Glendive—was solely his to dispose of, and no one else's. In a word, he hadn't paid taxes. Nor had he placed any credence in life insurance policies, and so upon his death, Laird & Sons Paving and Sealcoating was liquidated against his debts, leaving the family penniless. Agents of the state auctioned the Bridger home. Deborah and the boys were exiled to Billings, where Deborah took employment at a call center and the boys enrolled at Rimrock.

The sky was endless and stitched with clouds. Barry walked along, hands in pockets, breath fogging. Reaching Castle Rock Apartments, he cut through the fourplexes and horseshoe pits to Building 6, and climbed the stairs to 6D. Rhett was there, seated at the table in his sweatshirt and reflective vest, knuckles stained with tar. Rhett hadn't forgotten to wash his hands; they merely were stained no matter the washing. Deborah busied herself at the stove. To her sweater was pinned a nametag: DEB, SATISFACTION ASSOCIATE. She ducked, peering under the cabinets. "There's my angel!" she called to Barry.

He removed his jacket, sat with his brother. Their mother carried forth toasted cheese sandwiches and tomato soup in mugs, arranging the sustenance before them. Before touching a crumb, the family climbed onto their knees on the floor, heads bowed over chairs. Rhett and Barry had crewcuts, and heavily lidded eyes that looked, closed, about as they looked open. But they were closed now. Their mother had sharp features and pageboy hair that fell forward as she prayed.

Now the patriarch, it was Rhett who intoned: "Oh merciful Lord, bless the nourishment You've provided and bless the soul of our departed father, Martin. May You smile on our endeavors and forgive the wicked who besiege us."

"Amen," Deborah and Barry said. They assumed their chairs and ate.

The Lairds, gathering for a meal, believed in inquiring about each other's labors. Spooning soup, blowing on it, Deborah said, "Rhetty, they've got you at the Estates this week? The Creek Water?"

Rhett dragged a napkin over his lips. That was correct, he said. He was at Creek Water at least until Thursday. Though the job, he said, would've been finished last week if anyone at the company he worked for understood construction. Again and again, they were re-grading the same driveways. The supervisor on the job couldn't figure out his drainage, even though drainage, everyone knew, was the simplest concept in Creation. As with all matters construction, Martin Laird'd had the final word on drainage. Swallowing some sandwich, Rhett reminded his mom and brother of that example of Martin Laird's wisdom. "It's like dad said," he said. "Water's just a blind sinner, always running downhill."

But the company Rhett worked for wasn't Laird & Sons. It was an outfit from Helena that'd hired Rhett out of charity, after his father died.

"Did you educate this man?" Deborah said.

"What?"

"Did you teach him?"

Rhett shook his head. "I don't know what I'd tell a fool like that. He doesn't care where water goes. We re-grade driveways, he re-bills clients."

Deborah nodded. "He's a featherbedder, then."

Rhett didn't know what that was. Deborah said, "Featherbedding is a problem as old as Scripture. The wicked believe Creation belongs to them, every mote of it. Their language is greed. They shun integrity."

"That's this guy for sure," Rhett said.

"When your father passed, that business with the house. With the company. That's featherbedding of a kind. What belongs to other people ought rightly belong to them. That's what these vermin believe." She stirred her soup.

Rhett sat forward. "That's why I'm thinking just two months, Ma. Maybe five jobs." He tapped the table. "That's experience customers understand. Christian customers. And banks understand customers. They'll get behind it."

Deborah nodded. "That's what would be right."

Barry knew what came next, and now it did come. Rhett patted his brother's hand. "Laird Brothers. That's what it'll be called, and not a devil on earth will take it from us."

Deborah touched Barry's other hand, and briefly the Lairds were manacled together, each to each. She said, "What about you, angel? How was your morning?"

"It was fine," Barry said. Besides "Amen," it was all he'd said since coming through the door.

Deborah laughed. "Fine's how they grind flour, sweetheart. Tell us about your morning."

"It was fine. Really."

"How were classes? Did you submit your math problems?"

He said he had.

"What about your story? Did they read it?"

"He handed it back today."

"Well," Deborah said, "tell us about it!" She gestured at Rhett, who said, "Yeah, Bare, tell us."

"He said it was good. He liked it."

Their mother passed a crust through her soup.

"He said it was the best one," Barry said.

"Well. There's nothing else he could've said about it. You put such ideas in your writing, such invention…"

It was how Barry's mother always described his writing, his and Rhett's both. Inventive, she said. Artistic, uninhibited. Barry, guiding his spoon through his soup, recalled the long history of his mother saying such things. Specifically, he recalled mornings at their home in Bridger, he and Rhett following their mother onto the screened porch, where she littered the floor with notebooks, sketchpads, markers, pencils and crayons. Before they started, she pulled the cushions off the wicker chairs and threw those on the floor, too. "Get comfortable," she said. "You can't be brilliant until you're comfortable."

Barry, those mornings, would climb onto the floor, hugging a cushion to his chest. He'd gather notebooks and two or three promising implements. (He liked crayons that were ragged with chew marks.) Then, simply, he'd wait. Some days, his wait was brief. Material flowed from his hands. Other days, hours passed without his notebook gathering a scratch, even as Rhett, beside him, climbed onto his knees over his own notebook, writing into it savagely.

If his wait was long, Barry's gaze wandered. He rolled onto his back, considering the cottonwoods in the window, reaching their bark into the sky. He saw those trees now, as he stirred his soup, the Montana sunlight shattering down through them. He looked at the trees, or at the doorway to the kitchen, where his mother stood. She flicked a towel at him. "Back to work," she said. "I'm not even here."

The sun pivoted through the cottonwoods; Rhett, crouching over his work, muttered and grunted, tearing pages aside as his marker reached the bottom. Eventually, something would lurch in Barry, a feeling, and he'd roll onto his stomach, addressing the nearest blank sheet. Whatever his feeling was—and it wasn't the same twice—he allowed it immediate, unfettered passage onto the page. That page full, he obtained another. Occasionally, this produced documents like others Barry'd seen in the world, newspapers and the like. But it wasn't important that be the case. In fact, Barry couldn't have said what at all was important about the documents he made. The documents themselves were merely husks. His feelings were the fruit.

It might happen, on a given day, that his feeling involved the radiant cottonwoods. *Lyt*, might appear on the page, Barry's blunt pencil dragging out letters. Over the top of that word, he might write: *bloo skye, wud, bloo skye, leefs leefs*. In autumn, *leefs* might be descending. In winter, his page would read *no leefs arond*. Sometimes, writing *berd*, Barry wrote it lightning quick, crayon wax streaking across the paper.

On another day, his feelings might pertain less to trees than to the giants and ogres he understood had roamed the earth during biblical times. Feelings involving biblical times actually bubbled from Barry with some regularity. He remembered a day in particular, a rainy day in Bridger, when a biblical giant stumbled from his cave to confront the ogre who'd been eating his apple crop. Both figures had produced swords, and soon the air filled with crashing clangs and grunts and glints of reflected light, just as the page at Barry's hands filled with *sharp, pointee, lyt, pointee stab, yell, blud*. Penning these words—scattering them throughout the page, at varying angles, as the battle itself was confused and tumultuous—Barry found himself inclining over the notebook, spitting on the paper. It wasn't globs of spit, but a fine, sputtering mist that freckled the letters as he formed them. At first, Barry assumed it was raining where these monsters fought, just as it was raining that day in Montana. But then he understood the spittle was perspiration. As they battled, the combatants whipped sweat off their brows and arms, their untamed hair. *Samsin hare*, Barry wrote at the center of the page, twice.

Their lesson finished, Rhett and Barry presented to Deborah the sheaves of debris they'd produced. Sitting at the table, she leafed through their work. It was marvelous, she said. Evidence of unbridled, unsullied minds. She gasped, indicating a marker's daring swoop. "My stars!" But, what her sons had made was only evidence of their minds, and not the minds themselves, just as lifting a heavy stone evidenced physical strength, without the stone meaning a thing. Accordingly, Deborah Laird trashed her boys' efforts, or burned them in the stove. "Who's hungry?" she said, shooing them into the kitchen.

Only when they enrolled at Rimrock were Barry and Rhett asked to treat the pages they made as writing itself. As requests went, this utterly bewildered them. The writing was finished by the time they submitted pages—it'd happened elsewhere, at an earlier time—what possibly could be gleaned from the paper? It would've been no less perplexing for the gym instructor to examine the basketballs they'd shot with, to see if they'd used proper form.

Being in a higher grade, it was Rhett who first submitted an essay, and Rhett who first received a score: *F.* Very little else, in fact, was written on the paper. There was the red *F*, then an army of question marks coursing Rhett's meaning like swerving borzois snapping at a hare.

Rhett didn't know what to make of the markings—he didn't know what *F* meant. He'd never seen a question mark. Deborah, that night, sat with her boys on the floor of their empty apartment—empty, as they couldn't yet afford furniture. Her mouth was a tight line. Rhett's paper already was ash; she'd touched it to a candle, and dropped it out the window.

"What'd it mean?" Rhett said of the paper. "Was I supposed to make it like that?"

"No. You made it like you should've." Deborah gazed at the candle, wavering on the floor. "It means they're forsaken, honey. They're beyond Grace."

They were silent.

"You'll do not a thing different. Do you understand? If they require translation, we'll translate. But you'll change not a thing."

"Translate?"

"Do you remember in Acts, Rhetty? Acts 2?"

He said he did.

"'The day of Pentecost came, and there came from heaven a noise like rushing wind, and there appeared tongues as of fire, each resting upon its chosen.'"

"Okay."

"The Word enters fallen tongues, honey. It enters tongues, and isn't diminished."

"I think they want me to do something different."

"And you will not. You'll write as you always have."

Rhett watched his mother.

"You'll write, then bring it to me. I'll shape it for their tongue."

The Lairds sat together, breath mingling, just as they sat together now, at lunch. "Angel?" Deborah touched Barry's wrist. "Sweetheart?"

"Mm?" He'd not tasted his soup. His sandwich lay cold on its plate.

"What else did he say?"

"Who?"

"Your teacher, goofy. Your Languages teacher. Did he say anything else?"

"Oh," Barry said. "No. He just said he liked it."

Deborah squeezed his arm. "I bet he did."

The morning for Barry actually had gone this way.

First period, he'd submitted his math problems, as stated. Second period, Mr. Taggart had indeed passed back the class's stories, but he'd not said Barry's was the best of them, nor had he even said Barry's was good. There'd been no comments whatsoever on Barry's work, nor on anyone's. Papers distributed, Mr. Taggart had strolled before the class. Hitching his trousers, he'd addressed his considerable girth to the sophomores of English Lang II. "Well," he said, "good work on this little thing. I'm not kidding, either. There's writers in this room. Somebody wrote something about a poop that became a racecar driver..."

"Logan" someone groaned. The class laughed.

Taggart said, "Formula One poops have no precedent in American Literature. We're really exploring frontiers."

More laughter. Taggart hadn't yet looked at Barry, but now did, for a deliberate two seconds. He looked away. "So since these creations were so superlative, I decided I want sequels."

"*Uuugh*," the room said, slumping collectively.

"Now, now. You're about to climb back into your Narnias. This is an exciting opportunity."

Notebooks slapped onto desks. Several pencils escaped supervision, hitting the floor with soft clicks.

Taggart held up a meaty peace sign. "Two pages," he said. "That's it. Just write what happens next. I don't want anyone worrying about grades, either. A's for everyone on this."

Taggart remained there, rocking onto his toes and off again. The writing underway, he drifted back to his desk to score papers for another class. Meanwhile, all around Barry, students scribbled furiously, biting tongues and now and again dropping pencils, stretching necks. Outside, the athletic fields were deserted.

Barry's page was empty. His whole notebook was empty, actually, besides some drawings he'd made of crows and pigs. Climbing from his desk, he followed the aisle to Taggart's desk. The man's eyes lifted, fixing Barry in a blank stare. "Yes? What is it?"

Barry glanced at his classmates, then leaned toward his teacher. "I don't..." He remembered what Rhett'd told him about these situations—what you could say, and what the school had to allow you. "I just... get anxious. I have anxiety."

Taggart nodded. "And that's fine. Just remember this isn't for a grade. There's no pressure here."

Barry stared at the man's face. "I think I'm still anxious, though."

"You'll do your best."

"I think if I could... I mean..."

"Barry." Taggart removed his spectacles, and squared his face to the boy's. "You'll return to your desk, and complete the assigned work."

Barry tried to say more, but Taggart selected a paper from his stack and began marking it. Eventually, Barry returned to his empty notebook.

In the story he'd written originally—the one he'd drafted, then submitted to his mother for translation—detestable villains had abducted a fine king, envying his wealth and purity. The villains plotted assassination, but absconding with the king to a desert, they found him impervious to violence. Striking at him with knives, their blades shattered uselessly. And so, while the villains might detain this king forever, in the crude cage they'd fashioned, they could never end his life. Instead, the villains themselves would die in the desert, their prisoner watching them starve.

That was how the story'd ended. *Sand bloz desrt plas*, was written somewhere near the bottom of the final page, around which was written *heet wind thay r ded.* Taking up his pencil, drawing breath, Barry continued the tale. The indestructible king, villain corpses littered all around, takes hold of his rebar cage, prying it open mightily. *Lyf*, Barry wrote. *Aliv aliv. Free.*

When the bell rang, his king was striding from the cage, wearing courtly robes, sand whirling about him. *Jernee now*, Barry wrote, then added quickly, *bee brav r keeng.* Tearing the page from his notebook, he left it with his classmates' work on the podium, on his way to third period. Ideally, his mother would've translated the sequel, but Barry was proud of what he'd made. With luck, what he'd made would shine through untranslated, like sunlight through a leaf.

During fourth period, a student teacher fetched Barry from Biology I, walking him back downstairs to Taggart's room. Taggart sat at his desk, tapping a pencil on his knuckles. There was no class in his room that period. Barry sat across from him. When the student teacher left, Taggart said: "That's one imaginative assignment you submitted this morning."

"Thank you," Barry said, believing.

The pencil met each knuckle on Taggart's hand. He was a thick man with thick bifocals, a beard. He set the pencil aside. "Yes, it was a fantastical creation. I'll grant you that. But Barry," Taggart adjusted his posture, chair squeaking underneath him, "you are an illiterate individual. Is that something you understand?"

"What?" Barry said.

Taggart nodded solemnly. "It's quite true, Barry. You cannot write the English language, and almost certainly you can't read it."

"Wait," he said. "What are you..."

Taggart subsided in his chair, allowing Barry to continue.

"I can write," Barry said.

"You cannot."

"I wrote this morning." His hands danced before him. "I gave it to you. Where's the...?"

Taggart produced Barry's assignment, placing it between them.

"What's...?" Barry said. "I don't understand."

Taggart nodded at the story. "That page," he said, "is gobbledygook. You can make gobbledygook, but you cannot write the English language."

"Wait," Barry said. "No, listen. I write. Those are my..."

Taggart shook his head.

"Those are my ideas."

Taggart placed a fingertip on his desk. He didn't tap the desk. His finger simply stood there until Barry fell silent. He withdrew his hand. "This isn't a question of ideas, Barry. This isn't about anxiety. It's not a learning style. Reading and writing are fundamental abilities you do not possess." The man's eyebrows ascended from his spectacles, perching high on his forehead. "Do you understand?"

"But..."

"There will be no buts now, Barry. There will be no evasion. You need to accept that you are an illiterate individual. Nothing will get better until you accept that."

Barry was silent. Finally Taggart said, more softly, "You're Rhett's brother, is that correct?"

Barry didn't speak.

"Your brother was in my class two years ago. His mother wrote his papers for him. Now she's writing yours."

Barry shook his head.

"I would believe, Barry, that you don't know it's happening. I don't believe your brother knew. But Barry, listen to me. Your mother leads you to believe..."

"You don't talk about her."

"Well. Probably she leads you to believe any number of things. But you cannot read, son. You cannot write. These are facts. And no amount of believing..."

Barry left the room. Fourth period was nearly over, so he left campus and walked home for lunch.

Her sandwich finished, Deborah Laird pulled on her jacket and hurried to catch her bus. Rhett and Barry scrubbed dishes, Rhett sponging while Barry dried, put away. The mugs Rhett handed Barry were as soup-stained as they'd been before he sponged them; Barry toweled out the stains, placing the mugs on their shelf.

Rhett said, "What if we made it Laird Sons? 'Cause that's who we are, you know, we're dad's kids. We should make it Laird Sons."

"Who'd you talk to?" Barry said.

"What?"

"When they tried to give you those tests. You remember that? There was someone you talked to..."

Rhett turned from the sink, faucet running.

"I can't remember the guy's name," Barry said.

"Did someone come at you? Is that what this is about?"

"I just can't remember his name."

"I bet it was Miss Isaacs, huh? Goddamn." Rhett knocked off the water. "Woman's pure skank. She has three kids, you know that?" He held up three fingers. "Never been married once."

"It's not Miss Isaacs."

"Is it Taggart? That tub of shit?"

"I just want the guy's name, Rhett."

Rhett dried his hands, and crossed the room to his boots. "Dr. Avery," he said, jerking his laces. "Malcolm Avery. He's in that office downstairs. What you do is you go down there—hey, you ready?"

Barry pulled on his jacket, and the brothers walked together into the cold afternoon, eyes lidded against the sun. Rhett finished what he was saying. "You basically go down there. Guy's name's Dr. Avery. Just tell him what's true. You're not comfortable how they're making you learn, your needs aren't being met. All that shit. Dr. Malcolm Avery. Certifiable hippie, tell you what. But he gets what's true."

They climbed into Rhett's truck, or the truck that was becoming Rhett's at the rate of $116 a month. They drove along under empty sky, Rhett patting the wheel. "Laird Family Industrial. That's another option."

"That's a good one," Barry said.

They stopped at the school.

"I guess the name doesn't matter much," Rhett said, and Barry knew what his brother'd say next.

"Long as we get our fucking lives back," Rhett said.

Malcolm Avery's office was a cramped room adjoining a small waiting area. Another kid had arrived first, a boy with a caved chest whose curly hair began atop his head, like the hair of an aging man. He looked up when Barry entered, his grin toothy and quizzical like he couldn't see past his nose. He resumed reading the book in his lap, which Barry saw was one of those wizard books kids like this one always carried around. Barry sat in the other chair. The clock on the wall buzzed faintly, its second hand rounding off a minute. Elsewhere on the wall hung posters of mountains and oceans and kids of many races interlocking arms.

The kid beside him snorted, startling Barry. Looking over, he saw it was just the wizards. With his caved chest, the kid's nose dipped nearly to the book's crease. He hugged himself, grinning, working his lips on his big teeth. He snorted again, covering his mouth.

The door opened, releasing a girl with inky hair and bright lipstick, behind whom appeared Dr. Avery. Avery was a thin man, goateed, wearing a baggy sweater and bowtie. "Who's next? You?" he asked Barry. "You?" he asked the geek. "You? You? You? You?" His face swiveled back and forth. He laughed, waving the geek into his office. "You'll be next," he told Barry. "Unless I need a cigarette."

The door closed. Barry slumped in his chair, head resting on the wall. Behind the door, Dr. Avery said something loudly, then laughed. A bell rang, the office window filling with passing faces. On the chair beside him, Barry noticed the discarded wizard book. Leaning to see it, he discovered on the cover a geek not unlike the book's owner. This one rode a broom, scarf billowing. Behind him danced a unicorn. Glancing at Avery's door, Barry fingered the book open.

The page before him was flat lettering, an unbroken wall of it, and on that wall Barry found no portal into what'd made the kid laugh. He knew it was there, but running his fingers over the page, he found no seam. It wasn't the first time Barry'd done this. He'd even done it with these very books, which were everywhere. Closing the book, he studied its cover. The clock buzzed.

What he felt then he'd felt before—that something lay just beyond him, beyond his grasp—but he sensed now that this thing, whatever it was, was larger than he'd reckoned. Far larger. It surpassed reading, surpassed laughs in a wizard book. It was a wild, expansive country, within which waited everything imaginable, everything real. It was like the country lying hidden behind a rise of highway, but as Barry pictured that highway it became not any road, but the road winding south out of Bridger, Montana, toward what'd been the Laird home. And coming over the rise was the Chevrolet pickup that'd been Martin Laird's. The truck slowed, blinker flashing. Turning at the mailbox, it sailed up the driveway toward the porch, where Barry stood, opening a seam of dust.

Avery's door opened. The sickly kid collected his backpack and book. Waving Barry into his office, then walking ahead of him around the desk, the doctor said, "Bernard Laird, how wonderful to have you. Brother of Everett Laird. Son of Deborah. How is Rhett, anyhow?"

"He's good."

Avery reviewed a folder, then tossed it aside. "Sit," he said, "sit," and Barry sat.

"I remember your brother had a unique perspective."

"That's true."

"So. What can I do for Laird Number Two? Laird the Younger?"

Barry shifted in his chair. "I think..." he said.

"Yes? What is it?"

"I'm just," Barry said. "I guess I'm not quite... the way I think... my needs..."

Sun River

2015

On the morning of March 2, which was Kate's eighth day of work at The Electric City Motel, she awoke early, and awoke her daughter, Elena, and walked the girl by her hand down the third-floor hallway of Savior's Mercy Shelter. Other women and children passed in the hall, most of them barefoot and yawning, hair erratic. Kate was freshly showered. She wore the polyester blouse that Sherman, her boss at The Electric City, had provided her first day of work. It was too big for Kate. Below her collar, which she'd buttoned to the throat, the shirt was practically a poncho. She'd stuffed its tails into her trousers, though the trousers also were large; the shirt kept coming untucked.

In the bathroom, Kate stood Elena on a stool, helping the little thing brush her teeth. Behind them, in the mirror, women carried shower caddies toward the stalls, their robes ratty, some robes hanging open.

"Get your molars," Kate said.

Elena mumbled something. Taking the girl's wrist, Kate withdrew the brush from her mouth. "What'd you say?"

"I said I was getting them." Foam dribbled down her chin.

"Well." Kate wiped at the foam. "Keep getting them. Get in there with it."

Elena inserted the brush, scrubbing emphatically. In the mirror, her red hair reached tendrils everywhere.

"Them teeth are your little pearls. We're not losing our dang pearls today."

It was a gray morning in Great Falls, dawn leaching through a wet fog. Kate walked Elena down 2nd Avenue South, commuter traffic streaming past. It was dark enough still that city buses, passing in the street, were floating chambers of butterscotch light. None of the faces in the buses looked out. The Bachmans turned onto 11th Street, toward Elena's daycare. At the end of the block stood Super Donuts, a whitewashed shack selling maple bars and fritters from a sliding window. They passed it every morning. Elena yanked her mother's arm, like a miniature friar hauling the rope of church bells.

"You can go ahead and knock that off," Kate said.

"But you *pro*mised."

That much was true. The previous morning, on what was to be Kate's first payday at The Electric City, she'd promised her daughter the following day they'd eat maple bars at the red picnic tables at Super Donuts. That, however, had been yesterday morning. Yesterday afternoon, toward the end of Kate's shift, Sherman had walked into the lobby, passing Kate at the front desk, and kept on into his office, not saying a word.

Kate'd kept working, thumbing through the notecards the motel used to register guests. But her shift nearly was finished. Covering the cards with her hands, she worried a cuticle fervently. Finally, she walked into Sherman's office.

"Excuse me?" She tapped the door. "Sir?"

At his cluttered desk, wearing his burgundy polo, Sherman gripped the Sonic burger he'd purchased yesterday, which'd spent the night in his pup refrigerator. He wore a gold watch with an expanding band. Sherman Dodd: wet noodle of a man with high forehead and moustache. At the edge of his desk stood the yellow Tupperware bin that, earlier, ought to've contained Kate's paycheck. Twenty other checks had appeared, crisp corners lined in a row. But not hers. Now, Sherman's bin was empty.

"Sir?" Kate said again.

Dodd observed his new employee. He observed his burger, then with great tolerance placed it on its packaging. "What can I do for you?"

"Well. I just thought with today being payday. I guess, I'm not sure how to get my check."

A napkin tumbled from Sherman's lap, landing under his desk. Rolling his chair back, he swiped at it fruitlessly. From where Kate stood, in the doorway, no more could be seen of her boss than his hunched, burgundy shoulders. "You," Sherman said toward the carpet, "do not receive a check today. I believe I made that clear."

Kate remained where she stood. Sherman surfaced with his napkin, pedaling back toward his food.

"Why's that?"

"Why? Arrears is why. We discussed this." He resumed eating, cheeks bulging with bread and meat.

"What's that mean? That word."

He swallowed. "Arrears? It means those checks..." He nodded at the bin. "...were for services rendered prior. Up till a week ago."

Kate gazed at the bin. It was from an old set, the kind with wheat bushels stamped on the sides. The bushel on Sherman's Tupperware had faded, though. What remained of it resembled a middle finger, floating in a yellow sky.

"I been working here," she said.

"Yes, you have. Absolutely you have."

"I thought I got a check for that."

Sherman fitted his mouth onto the burger. Chewing, he said, "And you will. Relax."

She remained in the doorway. Behind her, in the lobby, the thong of bells on the door jangled harshly.

"You'll be fine. Just keep your nose down and keep working."

"Ma'am?" the man in the lobby said. When Kate didn't reply, the man said, "Ma'am, I'm needing a room..."

***

The light changed at 11th and Central. Kate led Elena through the crosswalk. "Momma, you *pro*mised," the girl repeated.

"That's right, sweetheart. Momma promised."

Super Donuts receded behind them. Elena became deadweight, Kate dragging her along. "You..." the girl whimpered, dangling from her mother's hand, "...*pro*mised."

Kate stopped. Kneeling before her daughter, she said, "Hey." Wiping the girl's tears, she said, "Hey, listen. Listen to me."

Elena's mouth sagged to her chin.

"What am I always telling you about promises?"

"I don't know," the girl said.

"Yes, you do know. You do. You know because I'm always telling you."

"They get broke."

"Promises are like juice boxes," Kate said. "They're just made to poke holes in."

Elena sniffled.

"Even promises your momma makes." Kate stood, patting her daughter's shoulder. "Now let's go."

They continued up the street. At the next intersection, Kate said, "Except for that one promise."

"I know," Elena groaned.

"Which promise am I talking about? I want to hear you say it."

"Momma always loves me. Momma's always there."

"Good girl," Kate said. "And that's the one that counts. Couple of donuts don't mean a thing."

Savior's Mercy Shelter was giving the Bachmans sixty days. That included food, underwear, towels, and toiletries. It included sheets and facilities for laundering sheets. One of the women, a volunteer, had given Elena a stuffed elephant and *Toy Story 3* backpack. Daycare also was included. The Healthy Futures Center, on 11th South, had awarded Elena a "scholarship," renewable as long as the Bachmans were Savior's Mercy residents.

As of April 3, the Bachmans had used forty-seven of their sixty days. April 3, on which dawn now broke, was day forty-eight. Depositing Elena at Healthy Futures, Kate walked down 2nd Avenue toward east Great Falls, and The Electric City. Like most mornings since they'd arrived in town, this one was foggy. But the days were lengthening, growing warmer. Somewhere behind the fog burned a white sun.

The motel stood in a vast parking area, its pavement upheaved, potholed, seamed with thistles. Eighteen-wheelers lined the edge of it. Nearer the building, under its eaves, were the sedans and pickups of individuals whose luck and dignity, running out, delivered them here. On the trunk of one sedan perched an emaciated gargoyle. Heels on the bumper, elbows on knees, the man rubbed his forehead with the same two fingers that held his lit cigarette. Kate passed into his vision and out again, unnoticed.

Inside, the desk was deserted. Meredith, who worked the nightshift, frequently abandoned her post like this, hours before the day clerk arrived. She got away with it. Sherman was her brother, or half-brother. Before unslinging her purse, before unzipping her jacket, Kate strode immediately into Sherman's office. He wasn't there. The only alive thing in the room was a screensaver floating in the dark—a succession of Pontiac Firebird photographs, and Chevelles, AMC Javelins. The Tupperware was empty.

"Fuck," Kate said. Of Meredith and Dodd, she said: "One leaves early, fucking other comes late."

In the lobby, she stowed her purse under the desk, removed her jacket. For thirty minutes, she stood silently at the register, staring at nothing. Now and again, she peered in the office at Sherman's Tupperware. "Come on, Katherine," she muttered. "Calm down."

Emerging from the desk, she passed through the lobby straightening this and that object—a tourism pamphlet on the rack by the door, an armchair someone'd dragged sideways. Turning the TV to local news, she placed the remote, with geometric correctness, on an end table. Her last task was brewing coffee. She poured grounds, water, hit the switch, arranged cups.

Having extra time, she prepped the notecards. When he arrived in the morning, Sherman liked finding the cards of delinquent guests stacked on his keyboard—he reviewed them with his Ovaltine. If there were partial payments, or if someone skipped on a bill, he wanted those in separate stacks. In the end, though, every card went in one stack, which he handed back to her. "Hunt these down," he said.

Meredith was supposed to do the cards, and hadn't. She never did. But Sherman never arrived punctually, so there was time to work through them. Opening the drawer, she lifted the stack onto the counter. Aligned as they were, corner after corner, the cards resembled the envelopes that'd appear later that morning, in Sherman's Tupperware. Kate inhaled, exhaled, started reading balances. "Just do your job. Do your job," she said.

The third card down was illegible. Meredith's hurried script had inscribed the guest's name right over the balance, making nonsense of both. "Fuck me," Kate muttered. Holding the card to her nose, then to the ceiling's weak light, she finally flung the thing, like a ninja star, across the room. On the TV, floodwaters dragged at a bridge. Kate smoothed her eyebrow. Crossing the room, she retrieved the card, carried it back to the desk. She studied it under the lamp.

A blade of sunlight danced off the door, bells jangling. A round man wearing a stained ball cap limped toward the desk, hitching his jeans.

Kate manufactured a smile. "Good morning, Mr. Palmer."

The man's forearm and paw plunked onto the desk. Under his cap, Mr. Palmer had meaty cheeks, gray-and-black stubble. He'd checked in yesterday, during Kate's afternoon shift. Nodding, he said, "They got you back there all by yourself?" Tobacco odors wafted out on his breath, a toothpick riding his lip.

"Just for a while. Mr. Dodd's running an errand."

"That's your shepherd, is it? Mr. Dodd? Mr. Doodad?"

"He'll be back any minute. Can I pass along a message?"

Palmer smiled, cheeks crowding his eyes. Pockmarks appeared on his cheeks, high up. "Well, honey." He pushed upright, patting the desk. "I guess the message I'd like you to deliver is I'm sorry you had to leave this little Waldorf Astoria unwatched for a minute. But I have a problem in my room, and I need front desk Kate assisting me with it."

Kate opened a drawer, producing a booklet of carbon paper tickets. "Well, Mr. Palmer." She clicked a pen. "If you can describe the problem, I'll make sure Lloyd takes care of it when he gets here."

Palmer chuckled. "No," he said softly. "I don't think that's how we're doing this. I think you're coming with me, so we can handle this together."

"What's the problem, Mr. Palmer?"

"The problem?" His toothpick danced about. "Let's call it my mattress."

"Your mattress?"

"It ain't sleeping right, Kate. It needs rotating."

Kate wrote a ticket for the mattress.

"Now why're you doing that? Put that away." Palmer covered, with his own hand, the hand Kate wrote with. "Shoot, at least come let me show you. That way you can write it nice."

Kate didn't resume writing. With Palmer's hand covering hers, she couldn't have written if she'd wished to. The man said, "Think about it, Kate. I don't imagine old Doodad'd like hearing about you giving me the cold shoulder. Shoot, a paying customer? Ignoring my needs?"

Kate studied Palmer. His thick eyebrows arched toward his cap. With an affectionate pat, he released Kate's hand. "Now let's go."

The morning fog had lifted, revealing a vaulted sky. The air was still, The Electric City's thistles stirring just faintly. Kate followed Palmer across the lot toward his room, the man limping some, his good leg hauling forward while his bad one dragged. In the street, a teenager on a bike swerved here and there. Audible underneath everything was the thrum of the air base's jets.

Palmer entered his room, Kate stopping at the door. Inside, she saw a catastrophe. He'd strewn his sheets, and spilled shirts, towels and beer cans on the floor. His ashtray, on the nightstand, overflowed with smoldering butts. The curtains were closed; aside from one dim lamp, the room was lighted only by the daylight falling in around Kate, and by the muted TV.

Palmer faced her across the bed. Smiling, he prodded the mattress with his hands. "Well. I don't mind telling you I had company here last night. My guest, she didn't like this bed, not at all. The feel of things is important, and she didn't like the *feel*. So we used this nice floor." It was evident where they'd lain, the sheets twisted there. Palmer removed his cap, clawing his scalp. "What're you doing by the door, Kate? You're letting the cold in."

"We'll get Lloyd in here to turn your mattress."

Palmer's chin dropped to his chest. He looked up grinning. "Isn't that just how it goes? How it always goes? Simplest solution right there in front of us, we go and make it complicated. Come in here, let's turn this mattress. Isn't that better? We'll handle this together."

Behind Kate, an old Lumina turned off 2nd, gliding toward the lobby. She glanced at it. The car parked, Sherman climbing out with his vinyl bank bag.

"Are you listening to me?" Palmer came around the bed.

"Lloyd usually gets here around eleven."

He smiled again, cheeks bearing their odd pocks. "Honey. Is it that you're jealous what I did last night? Listen. I didn't know we'd be in this room today. You and I, right behind this door. Tell me that, I'd save myself for you."

"That's enough."

"I'd be your blushing husband. Just imagine that. Take you right down on this floor..."

She left, crossing toward the lobby.

"Kate!" Palmer shouted. He laughed, shutting his door.

Inside, one of the maids, Celestina, passed carrying her check. "Buenos días, Katia," she said. The morning news'd finished, giving way to *The Price is Right*. The camera panned frantic faces, bright colors flashing, music banging the speakers. Light fell from Sherman's office.

She found him sprawled in his chair, hands folded on his head. NASCAR highlights played on his screen.

"Mr. Dodd?" The Tupperware contained orderly rows of envelopes.

Eyes fixed on the screen, Sherman said, "I don't like seeing an empty desk out there."

"I'm sorry about that."

Sherman nodded absently.

"Mr. Palmer, in one-seventeen. He had a problem with his bed."

"Well. I don't like excuses, either."

"I'm sorry."

Eventually, bored of NASCAR, Sherman rocked forward and pivoted toward Kate. He noticed her as if for the first time. "Well, did you help him?"

"I... well, he wanted... I said Lloyd'd be here soon."

Sherman nodded. "So you didn't do that, either."

She was silent. "Either?"

Sherman gestured at his keyboard. "I don't see any slips! I don't see any cards! I mean, what else do you do here? You've been here, what, an hour?"

"I'm sorry."

"Everyone's always sorry."

He consulted his screen, guiding the cursor around. Kate retreated, but then stopped. Biting her cheek, she advanced quickly, thumbed through the checks. Sherman reclined, watching her.

The envelopes were alphabetical. "Bachman" ought to've appeared near the front, but Kate made it to "Wagoner" without finding her name. She started through again, but Sherman said, "It's not there, Kate. I don't know what you're looking for."

The checks froze in her fingers. Eyes lifting—they were the only part of Kate that moved—she met Sherman's gaze. Releasing the envelopes, she stepped back from his desk. "What do you mean?"

"I said it's not there. You're not getting paid today."

She nodded vaguely. "I didn't know that. I didn't know that was the case."

"Kate." He leaned forward. "First off, you've got a lot of nerve sniffing around for checks, when I come in here and the *desk's* empty."

"The desk."

"Yeah, the desk. Where one hopes to find a desk clerk now and then. Then there's no guest slips here? Kate, Jesus, you've got to consider this from my perspective. A guy in my shoes might wonder what in the hell he's paying you for."

"You're not," she said.

"What'd you say to me?"

"I said you're not paying me. You haven't paid me a dime, Sherman."

A long silence passed between them. Finally, Sherman twirled a hand. "Taxes," he said.

"What?"

"Oh, it's one of these federal rules. You don't get a paycheck right away."

"I already didn't get a paycheck right away."

"I know that. Listen, and I know it's frustrating. They just need to . . . I think it's your social security number they need to process. Anyways, you'll get paid next month. You'll get all of it, too." He wagged a finger. "Though I should hold some back. I think you know that'd be fair, with your errors and such."

She stepped forward. Hesitating just a moment, fingers brushing her thumbs, she grabbed Sherman's bin, flinging it sidelong into the wall. Envelopes fluttered everywhere. Sherman skidded back, nearly capsizing his chair. "What in the hell was that!?" The drywall bore a notch where the Tupperware'd struck.

"You owe me two thousand dollars," she said. "Twenty-one hundred and sixty, actually. I've worked here six weeks."

"Were you not listening to a word I said?" Standing, he stabbed a finger at Kate. "It's federal fucking law! Grow up!"

She pointed back. "You're fucking paying me. Now."

"You think so? Because I think you're getting the fuck out of my hotel. That's what I think."

"Fuck you."

"You think I owe you something, hire a lawyer. Otherwise, get the fuck out."

"You wouldn't have paid me."

"Yeah. Well, suck my dick."

An hour later, Kate knelt in the Bachmans' room at Savior's Mercy, stuffing clothes into sacks. Into a smaller sack, she'd stuffed their toothbrushes, some bars of soap. A naked bulb hummed overhead. A small mirror hung over the dresser.

In the doorway, as Kate packed, appeared a tall woman in a denim skirt. Besides her skirt, the woman wore a brown sweater, modest earrings. Her hair was a bulb. "Where're you going?" the woman said.

Kate kept packing. "We're leaving."

"I guess I mean . . . where're you leaving to?"

When Kate didn't reply, the woman stepped into the room. "You don't have to go, Kate."

"Can Elena keep that backpack?"

"What?"

"The backpack you gave her. I'm asking you outright, can she have that?"

"Of course," the woman said. "Yes, that's hers."

Kate nodded. "We appreciate it."

There was nothing left to stuff in sacks. Tying the handles, Kate placed the sacks at the door. She began making the bed.

"Listen, Kate." The woman placed herself across the bed. "This isn't a place where we ask people to leave. Do you understand? I know there's that sixty-day rule. That's just . . . think of that as your initial stay. Yours and Elena's. We don't want anyone leaving till they're ready."

"I don't know how you like these sheets creased," Kate said.

The woman shook her head. "The sheets aren't important now."

Kate nodded. "I'll just fold them back." Finishing the bed, she crossed the room to her sacks.

"Let's go downstairs and talk," the woman said. "We'll work something out."

"Not everything gets worked out," Kate told her.

***

Hitchhiking had brought the Bachmans to Great Falls—one February morning, they'd made their way from Bozeman to Three Forks, then from Three Forks had progressed north along the Missouri River, through Townsend and Helena, until, like the river, they'd spilled from the mountains into a city on the plains. Now, hitchhiking carried them away again. From the Healthy Futures Center, where Kate collected Elena, they set out on foot down 1st Avenue North, crossing the 1st Avenue bridge, from which they saw rafts of geese huddled in the willow brakes along the shore. Their first ride was with a man hauling retread tires to Shelby, who saw them sitting on the I-15 onramp, and stopped, beckoning them into his truck. They left his truck at Vaughn. Getting from Vaughn to Sun River proved problematic, however. It was an empty afternoon, with long curtains of rain drawing north over the grasslands. Vehicles passed only every five or ten minutes, carrying drivers who seemed irritated at the prairie highway's interminable length, and who couldn't be moved to compassion by the sight of begging strangers, even if one was a child.

"Where are we *going*?" Elena demanded to know, sneakers scuffing the gravelly shoulder. Her *Toy Story 3* backpack drooped from her arms.

"We're walking," Kate said. And indeed they were. They'd climbed a long rise of highway; Vaughn lay behind them, in the distance, past which could be seen interstate traffic, snaking up the prairie like a train of insects.

A truck whooshed past, ripping at the plastic sacks Kate carried. She chased her thumb after it, then dropped her arm, kept walking.

"I'm thirsty," Elena said.

"I know, honey. There's snacks if you want them."

"I don't want snacks. Where are we *going*?"

"I told you. We're going to see your granddaddy."

"I don't *want* to see my granddaddy," the girl said. "I don't *have* a granddaddy."

"Baby, we've got to hope that's not true."

Ahead of them, across the highway, appeared a sprawling structure with green athletic fields surrounding it. In one field, a baseball team practiced its fielding, the white dots of struck balls vaulting high into the blue sky, after which faint bat pings carried to Kate and Elena on the breeze. The players scrambled this way and that.

"What's that place?" Elena said.

"It's just another place, honey." Kate peered behind them for approaching cars.

"But what place?"

Kate considered the building, the uniformed boys scrambling across the grass. "That," she said, "is a school. Long Gulch High School."

Elena squinted at the building. Eventually, they came even with a LONG GULCH ROPERS sign. "Was it your school?" the girl said.

"Oh," Kate said, "I guess so."

"You don't know if it was?"

"Your momma doesn't think about that place much."

"Were there other girls you knew?"

Kate stopped on the shoulder, gazing at the building. Then she kept on, leading Elena by the hand. "Yeah."

"Were they your friends?"

"They should've been my friends. I should've made them my friends," Kate said.

By the time someone stopped for the Bachmans, the afternoon sky had drained of light. They'd covered half the nine miles from Vaughn to Sun River, and Elena every few steps emitted short, chirping sobs. The truck sailed past them in the dark, headlights glaring, then flared its brakes, easing onto the shoulder. It was a black Nissan Pathfinder. Coming alongside the passenger window, Kate peered in at a middle-aged gentleman—a groomed individual in pressed, expensive clothes, the instrument panel lighting his face. "Well," the man said, "why don't you hop in? How's that sound?" Leaning, he popped open the door for Kate, then reached back, popping open Elena's door. "I don't have a car seat. You'll have to hang on tight," he said.

The Bachmans climbed in, shutting their doors. The man eased onto the highway.

"Well," he said, "where're you two going?" He glanced at Kate, then at Elena in his mirror. Laughing, he said, "Is that what I'm supposed to ask? 'Where're you going?' I've never picked anyone up before."

"Sun River," Kate said, nodding at the asphalt stretched out ahead of them.

"Is that up this way? I haven't spent much time out here."

"It's a few miles."

"Momma…?"

Kate told Elena to be quiet.

After a while, gazing out at the ocean of darkness they sailed through, the man said, "Truth be told, this is my first time in Montana. It's my first trip west."

"Well." Kate nodded. She didn't continue.

"It's exciting," he said. "I flew into Billings Saturday. I've just been driving around. God, what country out here."

They approached a Y in the highway. "It's left," Kate said. "If that's all right."

"I can go left."

They sped through the junction, headlights illuminating a sign for Glacier National Park, 130 miles. Though that was a right turn. "Whoa!" the man said, glancing back. "Did you see that? Glacier! It's on my list to do Glacier, I promise you that. I want to get up there, then do Yellowstone."

"Promises," Elena said from the backseat, "are like juice boxes."

"What's that?"

"Quiet down, baby," Kate said.

They coasted into Sun River, passing the Ramble Inn Bar, in its stand of dark cottonwoods, passing the Sun River Public Scale, with its glowing sign and arrow, as if the scale were a Riviera casino, and not an abandoned cinderblock shack alongside Montana Route 200.

They thumped over a bridge, under which, in the moonlight, swirled inky water from the Lewis Mountains. "I hail from Blacksburg, Virginia," the man offered.

"We can get out here," Kate said.

"Oh. All right."

He eased to a stop at the town's one café, its lighted sign advertising DAILY SPECIALS and PAY PHONE. Kate collected her bags. "Thank you," she said.

The man shifted on his seat, glancing from Kate to Elena and back. A queer smile bent his features, and when he spoke next it was softly, just to Kate. "Well, I don't really know how to say this. But a guy like me, out here travelling..."

"Get out of the car," Kate told Elena. The girl unbuckled, opened her door.

"Now hold on," the man said. "Hang on a minute. I'm not saying it has to be much. But I really helped you tonight. You were all alone. Just show it to me, at least. I want to—"

Kate left the car, herding her daughter past the café, into the trees.

Dawn leveled across the prairie, seething in the cottonwoods rimming Wally Bachman's property. Lighted so, the leaves revealed their inner veinwork, webs of it encased in mottled, chalky skin. Dew hung in the grass—long grass, that'd dampen a trouser leg—and glistened on the patio furniture forgotten in that grass, Wally's old set. Up the street, a neighbor's sprinkler snipped jets into the gathering day. Through the trees, one saw over grassy lots to the riverbed, and past the river saw wide pastures, dotted with cattle.

Kate and Elena'd slept in the garage, bundled together on the backseat of Wally's Plymouth. It wasn't the first night they'd passed in such circumstances. Indeed, over the preceding year, accommodations had often come meaner than this one, far meaner. They'd have knocked at the house, but arrived late, and Wally Bachman didn't stir late into the evening. Nor did he stir early mornings. Generally, Wally didn't stir much anymore.

Exiting the car, stretching, they inhaled the garage's stink of motor oil and cat waste. Sunlight streamed through the smudged window, illuminating jars of screws arranged on the sill. Under the screws hung neglected tools. Leaving the garage, they drank with cupped palms from a hand jack in the yard. They knocked at the house.

Kate knocked again. While they waited, an orange pickup passed in the street, its weather-beaten driver observing the prodigal Bachmans, come home for forgiveness or favors. Giving up, Kate opened the door, leading Elena inside, the house being no more locked than the Plymouth had been.

The front room was in immaculate order: carpets vacuumed, cork coasters stacked, afghan folded on the plaid sofa. On the walls hung dinner plates featuring biblical tableaux, New Testament and Old.

"Momma, I'm scared."

"No, you're not. You're young and pretty."

They moved up the hall. "Hello?" Kate called. "Dad?" They passed a pendulum clock. They passed a crucifix.

Wally Bachman waited in the rear bedroom, in a wool armchair beside the room's twin bed. The room was plain—actually, it resembled the room Kate and Elena'd vacated in Great Falls, at the shelter. There was the bed with its one pillow. There was a nightstand and lamp. The carpet and drapes were yolk-colored, giving the air a yolkish hue as well.

Kate stood in the doorway, holding her daughter's hand. Wally said nothing. He looked at, or past his visitors, expression serene. He wasn't so old, nor even in poor health. He was fifty-five and clean-shaven. He wore a short-sleeved oxford, buttoned to his throat, and creased trousers terminating at his shins. There just was nothing in his face, was all. Kate wasn't surprised.

"Dad, hey, it's me," she said.

Wally did nod slightly, mumbling something. Anyway, his lips wagged.

Kate ushered Elena forward. "This here's Elena Ann. Dad, she's your granddaughter."

From his chair, and from his infirmity, the man glared at Elena, then at Kate.

"Oh, daddy. We don't need your righteousness today. Not today."

Wally studied the girl. Kate squeezed her shoulder. "Go on, hon. Say something."

"He scares me."

"Well, he's a scary old wildcatter. That's why." Stepping forward, Kate pecked Wally's cheek. "Good to see you, dad," she said.

Elena sat in the bathtub, in suds to her armpits. Lacking toys for a bath, Kate'd fetched from the kitchen a plastic spatula and mixing bowl. The bowl was upturned on Elena's head. The spatula she used as an aspergillum, sprinkling the faucet while pronouncing some preschooler's benediction.

Meanwhile, Kate led her father into the front room, placing him on the sofa. She knelt beside him, covering his wrist with her hand. As if in ignorance of his daughter's touch, Wally gazed at the sunlight pouring through the window.

"Dad? Dad, are you listening?"

When he didn't reply, Kate drew and released breath. She said, "I guess you didn't expect to see me today, huh? You thought you'd never see me again."

Wally closed and opened his eyes. He wasn't ignoring his daughter. Ignoring was too willful an act, too deliberate. He just was gone.

Kate said, "Dad, I won't draw this out, okay? I'll tell you straight up: Elena and I need help. We're on our asses something bad, that's the long and short of it. You might think there's somewhere else we can go . . ." She shook her head. "There ain't."

Wally gazed at her then. It seemed he might smile, might even speak. He didn't. His attention floated away. Kate allowed her own gaze to wander, patting his wrist.

Outside, the screen hinges creaked. The door opened, admitting a squat woman wearing thick spectacles, a gray braid resting on her shoulder.

"My Lord," she gasped, seeing Kate. Closing the door, she indicated Kate with her finger. "I told them it wasn't true. I said that vamp wouldn't have the *gall* . . ."

Kate withdrew her hand from Wally's wrist, pushing upright. "Hello, Barbara."

"They told me in town. They said you'd turned up here. I said never happen, not in this life or the next. Even a wasteling like Katherine Renee has shame enough..." The woman trailed off. Stepping from the door, she pointed back at it. "Get out."

Kate didn't move.

"You will leave this house."

"There ain't a place for me to go, Barbara."

The woman's nostrils fumed. She seemed ready to speak when, up the hall, Elena squealed in the tub. Barbara glanced that direction, then looked at Kate, features remade. Wally, meanwhile, gazed at the window.

"I don't know what you want me to tell you," Kate said.

"There ain't nothing you can tell me, young woman. Young bitch. A *child*?"

"We ain't here just for pissing you off, if that's what you're thinking. We wouldn't have made the trip for that."

Barbara stormed up the hall. Kate followed. The old woman, in her floral blouse, stood in the light falling out from the bathroom, gazing at the giggles therein. Not looking at Kate, she said, "Is it his?"

"Whose?"

"You know who I mean. That addict you shacked up with. Lonnie."

"That's not his name."

"Is this thing his?"

Reaching past Barbara, Kate shut the bathroom door. Their faces inches apart, Kate said, "Barbara, that girl isn't a 'thing.' You won't call her that again."

"That's an illegitimate child."

"Her name's Elena Ann."

They watched each other. Barbara walked off.

Kate found her in the kitchen, opening and slamming cabinets. "Will you leave, Kate, or must I phone the authorities?"

"Barbara..."

"Answer the question, Katherine. Are you leaving this house, or must I telephone the police?"

"We don't have," Kate said, "anywhere to go."

"That's no concern of mine."

"Barbara..."

The woman folded her arms, leaning against the counter. Eventually, she said: "Go to your mother's."

Kate was silent. Then she said, "You know goddamn well I can't do that."

"That's correct," Barbara said. "You can't, can you? Don't you think there's a lesson there?"

"This has nothing to do with her."

Barbara laughed. "That," she said, "is where you're wrong, sweetheart."

Kate didn't speak.

"This has everything to do with her. One beast begets another." Barbara nodded down the hall. "Who begets a third, it seems. All of you bear the mark of it."

"You listen to me."

"I will not."

"We don't have anywhere to go."

"That's no concern of mine, Katherine Renee. And it's no concern," Barbara pointed through the wall, "of your father's. I don't suppose you considered his welfare, coming here? He's an unwell man, Katherine. He's made his peace with what you are. And now you—"

"Barbara." Kate's voice stiffened. "You aren't listening to me. We don't have. Anywhere. To go. We don't have. A home."

Barbara laughed. She seemed gloriously amused. "I'm afraid *you*, Katherine, aren't listening to *me*. You won't get a dime from this household, do you understand? Not a rusted penny. You aren't family to us. You weren't never family. I've always known what you are."

"You need to help us."

"I do not."

"Barbara, you don't understand what you're doing. I don't have anything I'm holding back here."

"No?"

"You've got to think about this. You're making this bad."

"*Bad!?* Kate, it's already *bad*. It's already *you*, can't you see that? It's *you!* You might could scratch out some money. Find a blind fool who'd pay for it. What's left of it. Wouldn't matter at all. Any leastways you slice it, Katherine, it's *you* in that soul. You, and the degraded bitch who made you. You won't escape *that* blackness." Barbara pointed down the hall. "That little girl won't, either."

"We need to stay here."

Barbara shook her head. "You do not."

"We need to be here till I find something. There's nowhere else."

"There's not an obligation in this world I owe you. And not a finger I'd lift willingly. I owe you prayers, I'll admit that. But I don't take joy in them."

"Barbara..."

"Go," the woman said.

"You're not listening."

Barbara pointed up the hall. "Leave this house."

"Do you," Kate shrieked, "have a *heart*?"

"And take," Barbara said, "that smear of filth in my bathtub."

It was, then, whatever object was nearest at hand: a glass pitcher upturned on the drain board. With a sickening *thwock*, Kate swept it across Barbara's face. Then again, again with the pitcher, till the handle broke in her fist. Then once with the handle, into the woman's neck. Barbara lay on her back, Kate straddling her, the older woman rasping as the younger panted. Through Barbara's fingers, covering her neck, oozed a red slickness, pattering onto the floor.

In the doorway stood little Elena. She was naked, her red hair coiffured with bubbles. Kate glanced at her daughter, then considered the woman underneath her. Bringing her face close to Barbara's, she said, "Where is it? Where's your fucking money?"

***

Leaving Sun River, the Bachmans followed crumbling highways, forgotten highways, toward the mountains west of Augusta. Entering the foothills, one gravel road split into others. Then that road into others. At such junctions, the Plymouth idled uncertainly before swiveling its tires up this route or that. It wasn't later than midafternoon, but passing into the mountains, the sun vanished behind them. Clouds streamed over the peaks. The last home they'd spotted was miles ago, an abandoned farmstead in the reeds near a slough.

Winding through the canyons, snow appeared everywhere. It was April, but snow'd persist there till May, even June, the floors of those canyons receiving perhaps an hour of sunlight daily, no more. The Plymouth's bald tires skidded and wallowed, its engine racing. They kept on, then floundered badly in a drift. After several lunges, a burning scent wafting through the registers, Kate levered the car into reverse, backing carefully down the grade to a turnout. They nearly floundered there, in the mud, but Kate pivoted the car till it pointed downslope. She levered into park, killed the engine.

Elena, in the passenger seat, squinted at Kate as one squinted at naked sunlight. "Momma, is that woman dead?"

"I don't know, honey."

Elena thought that over. "Do we want her to be?"

"Put your coat on, okay? Let's walk around."

Outside, the windy canyon filled their nostrils with piney, earthen smells. The Bachmans followed a streambed, watching river stones quiver under the current. Overhead, a hawk sailed thermals, rising and falling.

They walked till the canyon shadows, ascending, engulfed the peaks, then drove back onto the plains. Before Augusta, they turned north onto ranch roads, keeping to such roads till Choteau, where Kate gassed up the Plymouth and bought snacks. Leaving town, they passed a museum with a triceratops in its lawn. "Dinosaur!" Elena shouted.

Kate eyed the cars in her rearview. Scrambling to the back window, Elena cried, "Momma, stop! I want to see it!"

"Sit down," Kate snapped. "Buckle your seatbelt."

North of Choteau, the long sun pinned itself across rolling fields. They camped that night at Bynum Reservoir, near the boat launch. An RV appeared, its driver stepping out to admire the sunset. But he left, leaving the shore to the Bachmans.

Sitting that night on the hood of the Plymouth, under wild prairie stars, Elena said, "Momma, what's chasing us?"

"Ain't nothing chasing you, sweetie."

Bats darted overhead, reeling and swooping. Elena said, "What if it finds us?"

A wind gusted, tumbling their pretzel bag into the weeds. "Go and fetch that," Kate said. When Elena returned, Kate wrapped her in a coat. "Now. Which of those stars is the brightest?"

The Nielsen farm stood in empty country east of Conrad, east even of the grain elevators at Ledger—country from which nothing could be seen but more country like it. No town. None but a few widely spaced farmhouses with stiches of powerline connecting them. Grassy hills appeared to the north, but no mountains could be seen, there was no water, no trees.

Becky Nielsen came onto the stoop in her jeans and sweatshirt, filling saucers for the cats living under the house, cats that ate the mice. They slunk out from the crawlspace, three or four of them, lapping the bowls. Wiping her hands, Becky saw the car turn off the road, raising dust as it came up her driveway.

It parked, a woman and young girl stepping out, the girl wearing a backpack.

Becky shielded her eyes. "Who is that?"

"Becky?" Kate said.

"What I'm not getting," Becky said. "And I'm not *opposed* to this, but what I'm not understanding..."

"I know," Kate said.

"I mean, why us, Kate?"

"I know."

They sat at the Nielsens' table, coffee sachets steeping in their mugs. Sunlight streamed through the threadbare curtains, lighting the dust floating in Becky's kitchen. In the living room, Elena sat with the Nielsen children, playing a game involving painted blocks.

"I mean," Becky said, "and forgive me for saying this. But high school was years ago. And Kate, we wasn't friends."

Kate bobbed her coffee string, then released it. "I guess... you came to mind, Becky. You were always such a whole person. I don't know."

Becky clicked her tongue.

"You were."

"You mean whole*some*, I suspect." Becky flicked Kate's arm with a rag. "You mean boring."

"That's not what I mean."

Becky gazed at Kate, smiling faintly. "You never were boring, were you?"

"I guess not."

"Boy," Becky said. "I envied you. I sure did. You had spirit, Kate."

"'Had' is right."

"Oh," Becky said, "I'm sure it's still there. You always have your spirit."

Kate gazed through the doorway at the playing children. "I think all that," she said, "went into her."

Becky nodded. "Well, that happens, too. I'll attest to that."

"It'd just be for a while," Kate said.

Becky watched her. "It can be for a while," she said, "or for longer. Peter won't mind."

The women were silent.

"Is everything all right, Kate?"

"I think I'll talk to my daughter."

Kate went in the living room. Watching the kids, she tried to understand their game. One rolled a block, then another rolled, then a third and fourth. The colors that turned up determined who'd won. The kids howled, diving into the middle for their blocks, or for different ones.

The previous evening, before climbing into the Plymouth to sleep, Kate, under the stars, had said, "You know what I'm always telling you, honey? About juice boxes and all?"

Elena'd nodded.

"And you know that one promise? The one that's different?"

The girl'd sat there, huddled in her coat. She'd said, "Is that one getting a hole poked in it?"

"No. No, that's not it, baby." Kate pivoted on the hood, facing her daughter. "And you can't think that, okay? Don't ever think that. It wouldn't be true."

"Okay."

"I just haven't... I haven't been saying it right, is all."

Elena was silent.

"What that promise really is," Kate said, "is your mom always loves you. Do you understand me? And I'm always thinking about you, okay? You're my whole heart and mind."

"Okay."

"Do you understand? I need you to say you understand."

"I understand," Elena'd said.

And now, in the Nielsen's living room, Kate didn't speak at all. She backed away. In the kitchen, forcing money into Becky's hands, she said, "That should cover her for a time."

"No. You keep this."

"It's yours," Kate said. Leaving the house, she walked into open air, into sunlight. Into miles of spring wheat.

Afterlife

2017

I'm at the restaurant twenty minutes before Angie, who begged me to meet her, decides she'll show up. That's nice of her, interrupting my day then showing up eventually.

"Sorry," she says, collapsing across from me, her purse dangling, hair windblown. "It's just been..." She shakes her head.

"I don't really have time for this," I say.

"I know. I'm sorry."

I wave over the waitress, so we can get this going.

"How've you been?" Angie asks.

"Let's just have you tell me why I'm here."

"Don..."

"You used up all your small talk time."

The waitress arrives, and I indicate Angie. I already have my coffee. "I'll need a minute," Angie says.

"She'll have coffee," I say. The girl hesitates, looking from one of us to the other. She walks back into the kitchen.

Angie spends a moment watching me.

"What?"

"It's Connor," she says.

I shake my head. "Jesus."

"He's not answering his phone, Don. I don't know what to do."

"Stop calling him would be one thing to do."

"Donald, he's our son."

"He's a grown up, Angie. He doesn't want to be an adult, there's nothing we can do about it."

She's watching me again, with that *where's your heart, Donald?* expression she never learned has no effect on me. "Angie," I say. "What exactly do you believe is my role in this? Can we get to that part?"

"I thought you'd want to know your son is missing."

"Missing. Well, that's dramatic. More likely he's strung out."

She nods. "That could be."

"Do you want me to call him?" I take out my phone.

"I don't know if that's…" she says, but I've already dialed. The sooner I can dispense with this shit, the better. The call goes to voicemail, I hang up.

"I'm worried," Angie says.

"I can see that."

"I think someone needs to…" By the way she trails off, I realize we've come to the part of this where unreasonable demands are made of me. "What?" I say. "Say it."

"You won't like this."

"Say it."

"Donald, someone needs to check on him."

I produce my wallet, counting money onto the table.

"Don…"

"I think we're through here."

"How can you be like this?" she says.

"I'm not being like anything, Angela. The boy's made his decisions."

She's crying now.

"I live with it. He lives with it. You're the only one who can't let this go."

"I know that," she says.

The waitress brings Angie's coffee. The two of us sit in silence, except for my ex-wife's sniffles, while in the window a light snow begins swirling. It's directionless, the little flakes like blind insects that've forgotten the way down. "Fine," I say finally.

Angie looks up.

"Don't look at me. Just . . . I'll do it. Then you're going to leave me alone."

"Okay," she says.

I count the money again, then stand, pulling on my jacket.

"Thanks, Don."

"In the future, you need to be punctual."

The only times I've visited Bozeman were to drop Connor off, his freshman year, and then his sophomore year for a ball game. I remember it as a sunny town of restaurants and bars, with peaks surrounding it, but pulling off the interstate I find a gray, depressing place with muddy snow piled in the gutters. I can see just the footings of mountains, before they vanish in wet clouds. It was a six-hour drive from Spokane, which I made in five. I need to find Connor, tell him his mother's worried, get a hotel and get back. In two days, bright and early Wednesday, I begin meetings to sell my business interests. I've identified a single buyer who wants everything.

Angie's given me an address, whatever last address Connor gave her. I'm expecting to find lousy apartments, like those he lived in ten years ago—sixty units stacked and scattered over five cheap acres (the kind of apartments I built, actually, in Cheney and Post Falls)—but the directions lead past those places, past city limits, to a mobile court with a faded sign I can't read. The dirt driveway bumps over a culvert, brown water running in the ditch. The trailers are decrepit, if saying so isn't redundant, with ragged siding and smudged windows, the yards cluttered with damaged cars, toys. I look again at the directions. If the address were in a trailer court, you'd think Angie would've mentioned that. *Unit 8*, is all she wrote. I idle forward, arriving at a melon-colored place with a sagging blue porch. Blankets hang in the windows. Near the porch stands a ratty recliner with snow piled on it, and an empty pet cage.

Leaving the car, I walk onto the porch and pound the door, the latch of it so rickety I see, with each pound, glimpses of the trailer's interior. I pound a final time—no answer. Peering in windows, or at least the ones without blankets hanging in them, I circle the trailer, then again climb onto the porch. "Connor?" I shout. Vaguely, standing there, I realize I own this property. Anyway, I paid Angie when we split, and she probably pays Connor's rent. So, figuring I have quasi-legal standing, I shoulder open the door, popping it free like something spring-loaded. Inside, I find putrid furniture, discarded plates and Styrofoam cups, cigarette butts. It's no warmer inside the trailer than out. Strewn across the sofa, like cobwebs, are several oily quilts.

Eyes adjusting, I see in the next room, peering out at me, a bony face with long threads of moustache, under frayed cables of hair. "Who're you?" I say.

"Like, who're you?" the face says. "Busting in here?"

"Where's Connor?"

"Man..." The kid comes into the living room. Dropping on the sofa, he fishes a pipe from the cluttered table. "You need to respect individual boundaries."

"Who the fuck are you?" I say again.

The kid pauses, lighter at his pipe, then snaps on the flame, inhales. Holding his smoke, voice pinched, he says, "I don't need to talk to you."

I glance around, as if Connor might materialize out of the gloom. "Look, I don't have time for this. Where's my son?"

Through the smoke, and through the smoke's effect on him, the kid smiles at me queerly. "Son? Shiiiit, okay."

"Where is he?"

"I can just barely see it. You're like his dinosaur version. His avatar."

I want to break the kid's neck, but then am disgusted I feel anything at all. You know what, I decide: this'll do. I leave, walking off the porch. If Angie wants, she can drive to Montana and interrogate junkies.

I'm backing into the road when the kid trots after me, waving. I lower my window; he leans his face in. "What do you want?" I say.

"Man, have you..." He peers around at the weather. It's raining some. "Have you heard from Connie?"

"I don't talk to my son."

"Right," he says. "I knew that. But... well, I do talk to him. And I haven't heard from him."

The rain flecks my arm and pant leg. "Is that a fact."

"Honestly, I'm kind of worried."

A moment passes, the kid oblivious to the rain. "Has this happened before?" I say.

He shakes his head.

I'm thinking about Wednesday, about my meetings. It's 4:30 already. "Where do you think he is?" I say.

The place the kid names is a bar, which isn't surprising, but I wish at least it were a bar nearby. Instead, I'm following two-lane highways across tracts of emptiness, the low sky flat against the land. Here and there some sky drifts down, a tuft of raincloud, sprinkling my windshield. Where there's even spotty reception, I read emails from the bank, and from other interests relevant to Wednesday. A great deal must land correctly, in the correct order, for the sale to go off as planned. Then my phone alerts me: winter storm advisories, North Idaho and Western Montana. Hazardous road conditions. I scan the horizon, not seeing shit by way of a bar, just ratty brush and miles of fence.

Where one highway meets another, across from some grain elevators, I find a pinewood shack I guess is the place. Sitting in the parking lot, beside Buicks and rusty trucks, several of which are modified strangely—paint stripped to primer, or hoods missing, portions of chassis cut away with torches—I look at the scrap of paper Connor's friend gave me. In addition to the bar, it lists names I should mention, men's names. The kid was cagey about this. Writing out the names, he said, "Yeah, Connie won't really be there. He doesn't drink."

"What?"

"These guys might know where he is, though."

I looked at the names. They were all first names. "Who are they?"

The kid looked off.

"They're dealers?"

"Man, why would you ask that?"

I tucked the paper in my pocket.

"They know Connie. That's all you need to know."

"Fine."

"And you didn't get that shit from me, all right? I don't even know you." Even standing in his own trailer, the kid wouldn't meet my eye.

Memorizing the names, so I won't be reading them off the paper, I climb from the car, cross the parking lot. Without my noticing, night's fallen. The bar's neon lights spill across puddles.

Inside, the place is bigger than I expected. There's a bank of tables, past which stand pool tables, a stage. Beyond the stage, in the dark, one jukebox glows like a furnace. To my right, there's a long bar fronted by stools, on which sit eight or nine human backs. But the room's silent. On a shelf over the bar, a revolving Clydesdale spangles lights onto rodeo posters.

The bartender gazes over his patrons' heads, face impassive. I have nothing to say to these animals, and hope they won't make this difficult. "Evening," I say. The bartender nods. The drinkers are a wall of necks; none acknowledge me, nor shift to make room. Addressing the bartender is like calling over a fence. "I'm just looking for someone," I say.

"Lot of someones here," he says.

"Right." I'm about to try names from the list, but already I'm fed up with this trail of crumbs bullshit. "Look," I say to everyone there. "Does anyone know Connor Heinz?"

It's like I've spoken to mannequins. Nobody even fidgets.

"Splendid. You're all a big fucking help."

Now someone speaks, a rodent-looking man with a goatee jutting from under his cap. Pivoting on his stool, he says, "The fuck would we help you for? Who the fuck're you?"

My hands go up. "Hey. I'm not picking fights here. I asked a question."

"You'd better watch your fucking step."

"Derrick," the bartender says. It's one of the names from the list.

"Guy comes in here making demands," Derrick says.

One of the men leaves his stool. Crossing to the window, peering out at the parking lot, he whistles through his teeth. "My, look at that car."

"What is it?" someone says.

"I'm not sure I know what it is. Gracious."

Another crosses to the window, peering over his friend's shoulder. "Christ," he says. "Look at that. Looks like a killer whale."

"No one knows Connor?" I say. When nobody speaks, I walk to the door.

"Now hang on a minute," someone says. It's a man at the end of the bar. Crossing to the window, he glances out, then pulls out a chair from a table. "Have a seat."

"You know Connor?"

"Well," the man says. "Let's have a conversation."

"Don't waste my fucking time," I say. A stool screeches, Derrick standing and hitching his jeans. But I'm not worried. I know guys like these, I've employed them all my life. They won't fuck with a higher caste.

"Now just everyone take a breath," says the one guy. He sits across from the chair he's offered me. By the room's standards, he seems affluent, in a denim shirt tucked into jeans, tooled boots. He's older than the rest. "Please." He indicates the chair.

I sit. The man, thoughtful, brushes lint from his leg. "Now that's a Jaguar, am I correct? X something?"

I don't speak.

"I believe it's the XJ. And you got the long wheelbase on it, my word." He knuckles the table.

"Do you know Connor?"

The man leans back, appraising me. I slap my thighs. "Well. I'll be going."

"I suppose it's not a vehicle one acquires through patience, now is it?"

"Fuck you," I say. I hear Derrick moving around behind me.

"I know your son," the man says.

I wait for him to continue.

"Connie," he says, "is an unfortunate boy."

No human being on earth could attest to that better than I could, but I don't like hearing it in a stranger's mouth. "Go on," I say.

"He likes to owe people money. Me especially."

"So you don't know where he is?"

"Oh," the man waves that off, "I know where he is. He's hiding from me."

"But you don't know where?"

The man gives me a tolerant look. "Please. I know exactly where that boy's hiding. You didn't raise a clever son, I'm sorry to report."

I'm silent.

"I'm just letting him get worried enough to rob somebody. Get me paid."

"Where is he?"

"Should we go see him?" The man's face lights up. "Shoot, let's do it, let's go see Connie." He slaps the table. "We'll take that slick sedan."

It's one of those moments you can't comprehend. It's Monday; I should be organizing figures, getting documentation lined up. Then I should be resting. Instead, there's cowboys in my car—one beside me and one, Derrick, behind. We follow a dark highway toward, according to signs, Townsend, Montana. It was raining, but now it's just foggy, odd shapes of it racing at the headlamps. "On your left there," the older man says. I veer onto a dirt road. After a few miles, he says, "Radersburg, Montana. Home of Myrna Loy, if you can believe it."

We don't make it as far as Radersburg. The road enters some trees, where the man asks me to stop. Derrick hops out, passing through the headlamps on his way into the brush. "We'll give this old boy a minute," the man says. While we're waiting, he asks what my line of work is. I stare at the windshield.

"That's all right," he says finally. "People like us, we need to play our hands close. I get it."

"How much?" I say.

"Pardon?"

"What's Connor owe?"

"Oh, well that's a fluid figure. He owes what he can pay."

After a while, I say, "Don't get greedy."

"What's that, now?"

"There's a limit, believe me. I wrote Connor off a long time ago."

"Now that's not a very heartwarming story," the man says.

"Just don't ask for too much. You won't get it."

The engine hums, then subsides. I notice, just then, the stereo's playing softly. As if an idea's just occurred to the man, he slaps my leg. "Say, you ever hunted pheasant?"

"What?"

"Pheasant. Ringneck." He indicates his throat. "It's quite an experience, shooting them birds. They flush out of that grass, and *wham*. Tell you what, pull on ahead here. You'll see what I mean."

I look at the man.

"Go on," he says, shooing us forward. "About a quarter mile here. Get those high beams on, too. The halogens."

Leaving the trees, the road follows a wire fence into the fog. We pass an electrical box, and the shimmering eyes of deer in a field. Other than that, it's just fence and road. "Slow her a little now," the man says. "We're right in here."

We thump over a cattle guard onto two-track leading through grass. The car pitches and jostles. A rabbit flashes before us. "Little faster," the man says.

"What?"

"Come on, step on it."

I accelerate, the car banging off bumps and puddles, change rattling in the console. The road empties into a clearing, at the end of which stands a dilapidated shack, an old homesteader place folding like a penknife, most of its boards missing. Nothing in Montana matters to me, I'm there as a favor, but seeing that shack something falls out of my chest.

"All righty, here we go!" The man sits forward. I slow as we approach the shack. We're almost upon it when a side door flings open, a figure stumbling out, yanking on shoes. He hauls off after the long shadow my headlamps throw ahead of him, and nearly reaches the trees before Derrick steps out from the darkness, socking his mouth. The figure falls, lies still in the dirt. Whooping, the man beside me smacks my shoulder. "There you go! You damn flushed him!"

By the time I lead Connor from the bar, the two men watching us from under the eaves and Connor walking unsteadily, my hand at his elbow, it's daybreak Tuesday and has begun to snow. The highway, as we drive toward Three Forks, is discernible only as a narrow flatness in the white expanse. We see one other vehicle, a dump truck, then see nothing for miles.

"Take me back," Connor says, by which he means to Bozeman. That'd be fine by me. I'd take the kid to Bozeman, Billings—I'd leave him in a field. But I'm delivering this travesty to his mother. I'm placing him in *her* hands, after which she can deal with the violence and idiocy. Plus, Bozeman's in the opposite direction, and I have a meeting tomorrow and it's snowing.

Connor protests again, but feebly, and soon he's asleep.

After coffee in Butte, I'm feeling better than I ought to feel, given the circumstances, and can turn my thoughts forward. From where I sit, in my car, to 882 Ranchero Vista Drive, Palm Desert, California—where I've purchased a home, and will retire—there extends an unobstructed path, easily negotiable, like stones for crossing a river. I'll bring Connor to his mom, and that'll be all where that's concerned. I'll turn in early, then get to the office to line things out. By noon, we'll have an agreement in principle, and by the end of the week we'll have paperwork. I decide I want to drive to California. I'll hire movers, and just get out of Dodge. On the way down, I'll play Bandon and maybe Pebble.

Then: gin and tennis, and steak dinners, till the reel runs out.

Snow rakes the windshield like thrown gravel, riding gusts of wind and the drafts of trucks we pass, but west of Missoula the landscape slows, and is still. The forests grow taller, darker, the snow falling vertically now, as snow ought to, the plump flakes tumbling through pines. Scanning the radio, hoping for music from somewhere other than Montana, I find instead a recorded voice repeating the storm advisory. But whatever. We're halfway there. In the passenger seat, Connor curls like a fossil, his junkie limbs folded inward. Under his shirt, I see the skeletal ladder of his ribcage, and his ass, in his jeans, is just two bony knobs. His face is split, and it isn't clear what's bruise and what's blood. I think: Twenty thousand dollars this dipshit racked up to that meth cooker. I can't think about it directly without wanting to open the door, and kick my son onto the highway. I'm sure it wasn't twenty grand—it probably was half that—but when twenty thousand is what gets you out of trouble, twenty thousand is what you owed. It wasn't compassion that made me pay it, and certainly wasn't duty. It was expediency. Twenty thousand bought me never spending a dime on this pissbrain again, or even having to hear about him, and bought me passage to Spokane, where tomorrow I'll recoup that loss a thousandfold.

Connor stirs, his jaw parting. When I look again, spittle dangles from his lip. Like Derrick last night, I want to pound this weakling's face. To be hiding from his debts in a fucking shack, then the next morning, after daddy clears him, to be sleeping like a baby? I'll never understand that lack of pride, ever. And at thirty years old, no less. Just the same, watching my son sleep, I do see in his wrecked features the kid he was twenty years ago, when he'd fall asleep in the car, or at mass, or play dead on the living room floor for his sister to find him. And I admit it's a shame how things went for Connor. He did fine while we still had his sister—the four of us would eat eggs each morning, teasing each other some, before going our separate directions into the day. Weekends, we'd throw popcorn at the TV. Connor back then even asked me about jobs and things, what adulthood was like. I got to imagine him becoming his own person, he and his sister both. It was the two of them who'd carry our family forward.

Look, I don't know what impression I give. I'm not a heartless person. Lord knows losing his sister wrecked Connor. And then came his parents' troubles (it wrecked us, too). But things end, son. Families end. They stop, and afterwards you have to go forward alone.

The weather report's been the same message repeated—*winter storm advisory, hazardous road conditions*. There's been nothing about highway closures, but cresting a rise west of St. Regis, I see a mile of brake lights snaking up the valley. "Fuck me," I say.

Connor stirs. "What?"

We stop behind a minivan, the driver of which leaves his vehicle, pacing back and forth on the shoulder. "What's going on?" Connor says. Instead of answering, I hunt around on the radio. I check my phone, but there's no reception.

"Was there a wreck?" he says.

Leaving the car, I walk up the road to investigate. In all the idling exhaust, the taillights ahead shimmer like things underwater, though some drivers have killed their engines, their windshields accruing snow. In one car, a man naps under his jacket. Farther on, in the median, I see children flapping snow angels. I come to an eighteen-wheeler, its cab door hanging ajar. Perched up there, leg dangling out, the driver smokes a cigarette. His other hand holds a radio receiver.

I call up to him. "What's the story?"

"Got a truck up there!" he shouts.

Peering up at him, wet flakes land on my face. "How long?"

The man glances at me, then squints down the length of his own truck. "Oh, 'bout as long as this one."

I rub my lip, trying not to seem annoyed. Laughing, the man says, "Honestly, I couldn't tell you, pal. Sounds pretty fucked up up there. Started with the truck, then everything else piled on. It's up where the lanes split, so they can't get crews in."

I stare up the highway.

"Where you trying to get to?" he says.

"Spokane."

"Yeah, that's a common story. I'm shooting just for Wallace, and still won't make it. Shoot, I could as soon walk up and over on my own two feet."

I try my phone again, but there's no signal. It occurs to me I shouldn't have left Connor alone with my wallet.

"There's 200," the trucker says, considering his cigarette. "Though that might be closed too, I haven't heard. And it adds some hours." He shrugs. "But so does holding your dick in the damn snow."

"That's the road through Sandpoint?"

The man nods. "Yup. Head up from St. Regis if you can get back to it."

Returning to the car, I don't say a word to Connor.

"Where're we going?" he says.

Nosing up the shoulder, gathering speed, I swing into the median. "Shit," he says, bracing himself. Swimming, skidding, we claw into the eastbound lanes. I floor it.

Highway 200's a smart choice, because it doesn't cross a pass—it's all riverbank, straight into Idaho—but maybe 20 miles from the Idaho line we hit another jam of brake lights. Emergency vehicles ease past us up the shoulder, in no hurry.

I turn around, deciding we'll go through Plains, Montana, where there's a route north to Highway 2—it's three o'clock, and my phone tells me we can hit Spokane by nine, with the time change—but passing through Belknap, I remember there's another pass, and actually several, leading through the mountains to Wallace. I know this because we camped back there, years ago. And I must be exhausted because briefly I believe this is that camping trip, today; when we get into the mountains, Connor and I will grill hot dogs and swim. The fantasy dissolves, and I'm driving through snow again, my junkie son staring out the window. The passes I'm thinking of are almost certainly closed—they're logging roads—but if they're not, we'll save half a day. North of Thompson Falls, I turn into the woods.

Within several miles, I know I've made a mistake. The route's open, but not recently plowed, and negotiating curves I feel the tires, subtly, quit the road—momentarily, it's like we're sailing on clouds. There aren't other cars around, which makes driving easier but which feels like a message I'm ignoring. The snow falls, a sky descending as drifts rise to meet it, and we're losing light. But get over this pass, and I'm set for tomorrow, and for California.

At what couldn't be a worse time, with the road steepening into switchbacks, and me taking them at speed to keep from sliding backwards, Connor starts coming off whatever he was using in that cabin. It starts with a tightening—his body constricts on the seat, face pressing against the door. He unfolds and straightens, legs extending under the dash, then curls again, like a burning leaf.

"Are you all right?"

He waves me back, as if I were approaching him.

"Connor?"

When he unfolds again, I see he's sweating. The blood that dried on his face is once more glistening, like new blood; he leaves streaks of it on the window. Hands on the wheel, I keep my eyes on the road and on Connor, all at once. "What do you need from me?" I say.

"Forget it."

He's motionless, then sits upright, punching buttons on his door. He can't find the button he wants.

"Stop it," I say. "What do you need?"

His hands shake. "Fucking..." He hits one more button before curling onto the seat.

"You want the window down?"

Sweat stains the back of his shirt.

"Heat? You want heat?"

"Just drive," he says, voice quavering. "I'm fine."

He's not fine, but after a minute he wrestles his tremors into something manageable, a low boil he hugs to his center, like an animal he's captured.

I could say it's his fault, but Connor's episode has nothing to do with the last steep grade before the pass, which I see coming and accelerate toward—thirty miles an hour, forty, snow flying at the windshield, trees whizzing by—but which absorbs our speed easily, in maybe fifty yards, the passage of trees slowing, the snowfall straightening, till we're stopped cold. We slide backwards some, tires spinning, before I throw the car in park. I think we'll slide farther, but have wallowed well enough to hold. Dropping my hands, I gaze at the last twenty yards separating us from the pass, the car utterly still except for Connor's trembling. "Fuck," I say. "Fuck, fuck."

We should back down the slope, turn around. We should drive back through Plains, but going through Plains now would mean not making Spokane till morning, and I already lost one night of sleep. Plus I don't know that we could make it down the pass. Leaving the car, I trudge up the road through the gathering shadows. Indeed, this is the pass—there's a sign at the crest. Looking back, I see the car so close I could hit it with a snowball. I hear the dinging of my open door. "Fuck," I say again. After some rest—it's the altitude or the lack of sleep (or the being 68 years old), but this short hike has drained me—I start back down.

"Connor," I say through the door. I say it again. He peers over his shoulder at me, like a child awaking for school. "You need to drive," I say.

"What?" He looks around. "Where are we?"

"Take the wheel. Let's go."

Eventually, falling out into the snow, he shambles around the front of the car. He hugs himself, shaking—I can't believe how frail he is. He's like a dying little tree. "What're we doing?" he says.

"You're driving. I'll push."

"*You're* pushing?"

"Just take the wheel."

I walk around to the back of the car. Climbing in, Connor calls through the window, "What am I doing?"

"You're driving, goddamn it! Just drive!"

"Now?"

I plan to give him a count, but there's no breath for counting. Instead, leaning against the trunk, I simply push. Seeing me, Connor jams the gas. Wheels spinning, the car hovers like a planchette, then subsides into its ruts. "Do it again!" I wheeze, though I'm trying to shout.

"What?!"

I draw breath. "Again!"

This time, I push only briefly before my legs give, and I fall in the snow. The car slides over me, like a lid, under which the tires scream like table saws, choking me with slush. The recognition of my death is sudden and whole.

Everything's still, exhaust wafting around me. A door slams. Connor's ratty sneakers trudge past. "*Dad?*" he shouts.

I try to tell him I'm fine, but am too exhausted. There's hands on me; Connor pulls me out like a drawer. "I'm okay," I say.

"The fuck are you doing?" His ghastly face, hollow and bloodied, floats over mine.

"I'm fine."

"Get in the car," he says.

"We have to keep going."

"I know. Get in."

It happens dreamily. Connor helps me into the car, shuts the door. There's counting, shouting. I'm driving then. In the rearview, my emaciated son hauls at the trunk, neck tendons straining. I float up the mountain, evergreens gliding by. Connor trots after me, then falls in the snow.

We rest awhile, our faces and hands at the heater, before I put the car in gear and drive off the mountain. I'm clear now—except for one small pass, on the interstate, we'll run straight into Spokane—and being clear, I imagine the next few weeks, and few years. Going down there, I'll follow the seacoast to Pismo, along the grassy parts, then bend up along the cliffs, before cutting across to the Valley. At a roadside stand, I'll stop for nectarines. My place in the desert is perfect, a Mission-style rancher on the 10th hole of my club. I'm done with the Jag. I'll find something upbeat, a Carrera, then pack it with mothballs and drive a golf cart instead. The club down there has good restaurants, and a bar. Any clothes I need I'll buy at the pro shop.

It's a beautiful vector, shining out from that North Idaho wilderness, where the light's failing and the woods swell with shadows. But with the heater blasting, and with everything these past few days, I'm not feeling very strong, and frankly I don't know how far along that vector I can travel. Not very far, I guess is the answer. A little ways, but not far.

I'll rest tonight. I'll feel stronger tomorrow, and stronger still the day after. But if I'm not bullshitting myself—and I don't bullshit myself—this exhaustion didn't begin today, or yesterday, whatever day it is. I've been exhausted, truthfully, for a while now, and the shit in Montana just inflamed it. The inflammation will go down, sure. I'll feel better. But the exhaustion itself isn't going anywhere. It's like seepage into the walls of a home: it's not fast, but only flows one direction. I'm 68 years old. And it's not just me it's happening to. Three months ago, on what would've been our girl's 26th birthday, I went to Angie's house for breakfast (a tradition), and the same thing's happening to the woman who was my wife. She's moving slower, and the house she's kept fashionable all these years, updating everything all the time, has slipped into that near past, the way old people's houses do. It's the fashionable of yesterday.

Connor's trembling again, huddling at the heater as if it were a campfire. "You all right, son?" I say. He shrugs, rubbing his palms together. I don't know how serious his problems are, if they're the kind of thing a person can get over. But it occurs to me then: any continuance any of us has, is his.

The turnoff for the campground is gated, marked with prohibitive signs, but I stop in the road, gazing back through the trees at all the stillness back there, at all the silence and snow. Connor blows in his hands. "What're we doing?" he says.

"We had a weekend here."

I don't think he's heard me.

"It was the two of us," I say. "And your mom and your sister."

2018

The military had abandoned the compound decades ago, in the seventies, after the signing of this or that treaty. The construction on it hadn't progressed far. All they'd managed was a massive capped foundation set on the plains east of Ledger, Montana, a low gray profile under a sometimes gray sky. The supports of what would've been upper floors reached fruitlessly into empty air, like gray arms from which the hands had been lopped. The concrete walls of the structure were several feet thick. It was as if, at the President's pen stroke upon the treaty, the hundreds of workers who'd been enlisted in the building's construction had all dropped their hammers, walked off into the grass.

Now, barn swallows and wrens swooped in and out of the compound's orifices. Graffiti was everywhere, brash declarations of anger alongside crude depictions of genitalia, pouting mouths, middle fingers. Scattered across the floor were remnants of bonfires and what misbehavior had transpired at those fires—bottles, needles, the packaging of condoms from the clinic in Havre. Through all of which miscellany there moved, now, several solemn children. One of them, a boy, lifted a charred pallet then set it down again. Others peered in what would've become an elevator shaft, but which now housed only a mound of excavated soil, loose rock. It was believed by these children, and by all children on the surrounding farms, that the forgotten bunker was a dwelling of ghosts. Ranch wives who'd hanged themselves. Drifters from off the highline who'd frozen to death in blizzards. A wind kicked up, howling in among the structure's forms, trailing wisps of silt. One of the children screamed. Racing to his side, feet splashing through murky puddles, the other children discovered their companion in one of the bunker's shadowy corners, standing before a heap of small dogs. They were dead coyotes, or at least the musculatures of coyotes, left there by whoever'd salvaged the hides. One of the children crept forward, hand extended to touch a carcass, but it was then a voice was heard in the complex, a ragged, savage voice echoing off the concrete walls. At any rate, one of the children believed he heard a voice. Screaming, he hauled through the decaying space, the others running behind.

Outside, the summer air'd turned cool in the wind, the fields of wheat flattening madly in gusts of it, flattening and righting again, tearing at their roots. A darker sky stood to the east. Mounting their bicycles, the children pedaled west, pumping frames knee to knee. The rain gained on them, drops of it splashing their arms and necks. Farther back in the storm, one white stab of lightning stood briefly on the horizon. Then there was another, the rumbling of thunder overtaking the children.

But emerging from their midst, pedaling the hardest, was one child in particular, a small child, whose red hair streamed behind her. And the rumbling of that dark thunder was all that'd catch her. She pedaled faster, faster still, her companions receding. Ahead, on a low rise, stood the white farmhouse toward which she hurried. And her skin was dry, her hair dry: she raced ahead of the storm.

Acknowledgments

Amy, Brady, Mom, Dad, Joe and the Cincinnickols, Andy, Alec, Eric, and Damber—not once in my life have any of you expected an explanation from me. You've taken me as you've found me, and it's been the most freeing gift I can imagine. Thank you.

Thanks as well to Diane Goettel and Black Lawrence Press, who've shown such enthusiasm, patience and encouragement. This book at most is a down payment on that—I remain indebted. Finally, so many people along the line picked up these stories, who didn't have to. Without you, this book never makes it out the door.

Photo: Amy Scheck

Ben Nickol's previous books are *Adherence* (2016) and *Where the Wind Can Find It* (2015). His stories and essays have appeared widely, in *Alaska Quarterly Review*, *Boulevard*, *Redivider*, *Crab Orchard Review*, *Fourth Genre* and elsewhere. He lives with his family in Kansas, and teaches at Wichita State University.